W9-BSM-906

Whatever After

BEAUTY QUEEN

Read all the Whatever After books!

Whatever After

BEAUTY QUEEN

SARAH MLYNOWSKI

 Scholastic Press/New York

Library of Congress Cataloging-in-Publication Data

Mlynowski, Sarah, author.
Beauty queen / Sarah Mlynowski. — First edition.
pages cm. — (Whatever after ; 7)
Summary: Abby's first problem is that Jonah has lost all his memories of the magic mirror and their adventures, so when they get sucked through into Beauty and the Beast, he is unaware of the danger, and picks one of the Beast's roses—her second problem is locating Beauty and performing a match-making miracle in order to recover her brother, and still make it back to the real world before their parents miss them.
ISBN 978-0-545-74654-0 (jacketed hardcover) 1. Beauty and the beast (Tale)—
Juvenile fiction. 2. Fairy tales—Adaptations—Juvenile fiction. 3. Magic
mirrors—Juvenile fiction. 4. Brothers and sisters—Juvenile fiction. 5. Amnesia—
Juvenile fiction. [1. Characters in literature—Fiction. 2. Fairy tales—Fiction.
3. Magic—Fiction. 4. Brothers and sisters—Fiction. 5. Amnesia—Fiction.] I. Title.
II. Series: Mlynowski, Sarah. Whatever after ; 7.
PZ7.M7135Be 2015
813.6—dc23
[Fic]
2014049329

10 9 8 7 6 5 4 3 2   15 16 17 18 19

Printed in the U.S.A.   23
First edition, May 2015

for

penny fransblow,
queen of librarians

and

gabriella dylan friedman,
princess and future reader

* chapter one *

Come Back, Memories, Come Back!

"Put on your sneakers."

My brother, Jonah, hides under his covers. "Not again, Abby. It's already midnight!"

"Yes, again," I say. "And it's not midnight yet. We still have three minutes."

"But I don't want to sneak into the basement again! I want to go back to sleep!"

"Do you remember anything about our magic mirror yet?" I ask, looming over his bed.

"No," he says, his voice muffled. "Nothing."

"Then you can't go back to sleep. Let's go, let's go!"

Here's the thing.

We have a magic mirror in our basement.

And, at midnight, when we knock on it three times, the magic mirror sucks us inside and takes us into a fairy tale. Really. Well, first it turns purple, then it starts to hiss and swirl, and then it sucks us into a fairy tale.

The issue right now is that my brother doesn't believe that the mirror in the basement is magical. Which makes no sense because he has been through the magic mirror with me SIX times already. But the last time we went through, the fairy who lives inside the mirror — her name is Maryrose — hypnotized Jonah by accident.

He remembers everything else about his life — his name, my name, the fact that we live in Smithville — but he doesn't remember *any* of our trips.

At all.

Not even a little bit.

How sad is that?

We've had all these adventures and he has no clue about any of them. We hiked with Snow White! We baked brownies with Cinderella! He turned into a human Popsicle in the story of *The Snow Queen*! And he remembers nothing. NOTHING!

It makes me feel kind of lonely.

"Come on!" I whisper-yell. I can't be too loud. My parents are sleeping. "Let's go!"

I'm *really* hoping his memories come back once he sees the mirror in action.

Nothing else I've tried has worked. I made him wear his soccer cleats around the house. I was hoping he'd remember how wearing them had totally messed up Rapunzel's hair and left me no choice but to give her an extreme haircut.

I fed him apples, hoping he'd remember meeting Snow White.

I even showed him the jewelry box in my room. The paintings on the box show what happens to all the fairy tale characters after we visit their stories. Like Rapunzel with her shorter hairdo.

But nothing has worked. He still has no memories of our adventures.

"When did you get so annoying?" my brother mutters as he climbs out of bed and smushes his feet into his sneakers.

Prince, our dog, nuzzles his nose against Jonah's heel.

I ignore the question. "Are you wearing your watch?" I ask. A watch from home is the only way to keep track of the time when we're in fairy tales.

"Yes," he grumbles.

"Good. Follow me." I head down the stairs to our basement. "Quietly."

I don't want my parents to wake up. They don't know about the magic mirror. Maryrose hypnotized *their* memories away on purpose. Plus, we promised them that we wouldn't go into the basement at night, and I hate breaking promises. But what else can I do? I need Jonah to remember everything that happened and this is the only way. Also, going through the mirror is fun.

Prince follows right behind me. I can hear Jonah grumbling to himself behind Prince.

"Close the basement door," I tell Jonah as we climb down the final flight of stairs.

He does. I motion for him to come closer and face the mirror.

The mirror is about twice the size of me. The frame is made of stone and decorated with carvings of small fairies with wings and wands. The glass part is clear and smooth, and inside we can see our reflections. My shoulder-length curly dark hair. My small, scrawny brother and his messy brown hair. Prince's furry little body.

I knock on the mirror. Once. Twice. Three times.

I hold my breath.

Nothing happens.

No spinning. No purple. No hissing.

"Crumbs," I mutter.

I've dragged Jonah down to the basement every night for the past week to knock on the mirror.

And Maryrose is still not letting us in.

Why not? I have no idea. Sometimes she's picky like that. Sometimes she waits for us to wear certain outfits before letting us into the mirror, like pajamas that look like a kingdom's flags. But she doesn't tell us what she wants us to wear, and it's hard to guess.

A few days ago, I wore ballet slippers in case she was hoping to bring us inside the story of *The Twelve Dancing Princesses*. Today I have bread crumbs in my hoodie pocket in case she is thinking of taking us into *Hansel and Gretel*.

Between the bread crumbs and the ballet slippers and the apples, I have been working with a lot of different fairy tale props lately.

"Let me try one more time," I tell my brother.

"No," he says and scrunches up his face. "Enough. We don't have a magic mirror!"

"Yes, we do! What time is it?"

"Twelve-oh-five," Jonah says, glancing at his watch.

Double crumbs. "I guess it's not happening tonight. It's too late now." I exhale a super-loud, super-annoyed sigh. "We'll try again tomorrow."

Prince paws the mirror. He gets it. He wants Jonah to remember, too, I can tell.

"Can't we take a few nights off?" Jonah asks. "It's Mom's birthday on Wednesday. I don't have a present for her yet."

"You can share mine," I say. I made a painting for my mother in art class. It's of a vase of roses. Mom *loves* roses. I'm feeling guilty for sneaking around the house at night, and I hope that giving Mom something she really likes will make me feel better.

I'm pretty sure she'll like the painting. It's great. At least I think it's great. I'll know tomorrow when it's dry.

"Let me try knocking *one more time*," I say. "Just in case."

"No, no, no," Jonah says. "I don't want to talk to mirrors anymore."

"Just one more —"

"No!" he snaps. "You're starting to freak me out, Abby! We don't have a magic mirror! If you don't stop bugging me about it, I'm going to tell Mom and Dad you've gone crazy!"

"Wait, Jonah. Don't go." He has to remember! I need him to remember! "Let me get you a snack. Do you want another apple? A brownie? Or maybe a Popsicle?"

Prince wags his tail. Jonah blocks his ears and rushes up the stairs.

I guess he's not hungry.

* chapter two *

Swoosh

the next day in art class, I discover I was wrong about my painting.

It did not come out great. It did not come out great at all.

I pick up my painting from the drying rack and slump down at the long table.

My roses do not look like roses. They look like red blobs. Red blobs that were dropped on the floor and then jumped on with Jonah's soccer cleats.

"Good try, Abby," Mrs. Becker tells me, standing over my shoulder.

Good try? GOOD TRY?

Everyone knows *good try* means *you have no talent.*

The truth is, she's right. I am not good at painting. Or drawing. Or anything involving clay, either.

Frankie, Robin, and Penny all sit down beside me.

Frankie and Robin are my best friends.

Penny is Robin's other best friend. She hogs Robin as often as she can. And I'm pretty sure she's forcing Robin to wear a super-high ponytail to school every day so the two of them can match. The other day at recess, she referred to them as "twinsies." Which, even with the ponytails, is impossible because Penny's hair is blond and Robin's is strawberry-blond, almost red. So there.

I prefer to wear a headband to school, thank you very much. And Frankie is wearing her dark hair back in two French braids. Frankie and I don't *need* to wear matching hairdos to prove we're best friends.

"Wow, Penny," Mrs. Becker says, interrupting my thoughts. "The detail in your painting is exquisite."

Exquisite? Really?

I look down at Penny's painting.

I gasp.

It *is* exquisite. Seriously. Her roses are red and bright and beautiful. Her painting looks like an ad for Mother's Day, if Mother's Day needed an ad.

"That's amazing," Robin coos to her.

"It really is," says Frankie. "Where did you learn to be such a great artist?"

I swallow the lump in my throat. Sure, Penny's good at art, but it's not like she's a superstar at *everything*.

"I've always loved to paint and draw," Penny says, dipping her paintbrush into her glass of water to clean it and wagging her ponytail from side to side. "It comes very naturally to me."

I roll my eyes. I can't help it.

Robin and Frankie spend the rest of class fawning over Penny the Great. Penny *the artiste*. Penny the Picasso.

Who cares if she's good at art and I'm not anyway? It's not like I want to be a painter when I grow up. I'm going to be a judge. And you definitely don't need to know how to paint roses to be a judge. You need to be smart and . . . judgy.

I spend the rest of class trying to salvage the blobby mess in front of me.

"I just have to sign it and I'm done," Penny says after a while.

She dips her brush in the black paint and writes her name with an annoying flourish.

"That painting could be worth a million dollars one day," Robin says seriously.

I resist the urge to vomit. Although maybe if I threw up all over Penny's precious painting, I wouldn't have to look at it anymore?

Frankie and Robin pick up their paintings to put on the drying rack, but Penny leaves hers to set a minute longer. Then she goes to wash her hands at the sink near Mrs. Becker's desk. I stay where I am and stare at my painting next to Penny's.

I hate mine.

I love hers.

No. I hate hers.

Penny's glass of water is really close to her painting.

Really close.

Too close.

And that's when it happens. I knock the glass of water with my elbow.

On purpose.

Whoosh! Swoosh! The water gushes across Penny's painting.

My heart stops. *What did I do?*

The colors mix. The paint runs. The petals melt into the leaves, which melt into the vase.

Oh no oh no oh no OH NOOOOOOOOOOOOO!

Maybe nobody will notice?

I hear a loud shriek.

"MY PAINTING!"

Crumbs. She noticed.

Penny runs over to our table. "Help!" she cries. "There's water all over my paper! I need paper towels! Help! My painting is drowning!"

Robin and Frankie rush to get napkins and we all quickly blot the painting. But it's hopeless. When we remove the paper towels, all that's left is a blob of colors. A blob that looks worse than my blobs. Much worse.

"My painting," Penny whimpers.

"Poor Penny," Robin says, giving her a big hug.

"It was so beautiful," Frankie says, also giving her a hug.

"I'm so sorry," Mrs. Becker says mournfully. "Maybe we can fix it. Let me find more paper towels."

"I can't believe it," says Penny. She turns to me. "Abby, did you see what happened?"

My cheeks heat up. "I . . . um . . . It's my fault. It was an accident. I knocked over your water. I'm sorry."

"By accident?" Penny asks skeptically.

"Of course by accident," I lie. "Why would I pour water on your painting on purpose?"

She looks at me with suspicion.

So do Robin and Frankie.

It wasn't my fault! Okay, it was my fault, but not really, because Penny drove me to it with her *twinsies* and her perfect painting and her hogging my friend!

I feel sick.

What kind of person ruins someone else's art project?

A horrible person.

Am I a horrible person?

I swallow the huge lump in my throat.

My verdict: Guilty as charged.

✳ chapter three ✳

Attack of the Roses

a giant rose is hitting me over the head.

"You're a monster!" the rose is yelling, its petals twisting into lips. "A green-eyed monster!"

"Abby! You're screaming!" another rose yells in my ear.

"No, I'm not!" I scream back.

But now I realize I'm actually sitting up in my bed. Jonah is standing next to me. It's the middle of the night.

"What happened?" I ask.

"You were screaming in your sleep," my brother says.

My heart races. "I was?"

"Yeah. A lot. I could hear you through the wall. Something about a green-eyed monster."

Prince jumps onto my bed and nuzzles my stomach.

I was having a nightmare. Penny's roses were attacking me.

My checks flush. They were calling me a green-eyed monster. That's an expression my nana uses. *Green-eyed monster* means jealousy. The rose was right. I guess I deserve my nightmare after what I did to Penny's painting.

I *am* a monster. A jealous, green-eyed monster.

"Are we going?" Jonah asks me.

"Where?" I ask with a heavy heart.

"Downstairs," he says. "It's eleven fifty-eight."

I sit up straight. "I thought you were done with the mirror?"

He shrugs. "I'm awake anyway. If it doesn't work, can we play flying crocodile?"

"Now?" Flying crocodile is a game my brother made up. It's about crocodiles that fly.

"Yeah. I didn't get to play anything today. Mom and Dad made me practice my reading all night." He sounds grumpy.

Jonah's teacher recently told my parents that he's a bit behind the rest of his class with his reading, so they're trying to help him. He'd rather they help him with something else instead. Like playing flying crocodile.

"Okay, let's go," I say, jumping out of bed. I pretend I don't see the painting for my mom on my desk, wrapped in tissue paper. I wish I didn't have to give it to her. Not only is it terrible, but it reminds me of what I did to Penny's painting.

I look at my closet. Should I change? Nah. I'll leave on my flannel pajamas in case Maryrose wants to take us into *The Princess and the Pea.* If we do end up there, I could take a nap on one of those twenty mattresses. I yawn. That nightmare did not leave me feeling well rested.

Jonah's wearing his flannel pajamas, too.

"You stay here, Prince," I say, and try to close my door with him inside my room.

He barks.

"Shh!" I say. "Come on, Prince, you caused us a lot of problems last time we went through the mirror!"

Going into fairy tales is really fun, but can also be dangerous. And there's no reason for Prince to come along and wreak havoc.

He barks again. Loudly.

"He's going to wake up Mom and Dad," Jonah says.

Uch. He is. I open the door. "Okay, fine," I say. "Let's go. Jonah, do you even remember where Prince came from?" I ask.

Jonah's forehead wrinkles in concentration. "Did we get him from the shelter?"

"Not even close. A fairy in *Sleeping Beauty* waved her wand, and Prince appeared."

"Sure he did," Jonah says. Even in the dark, I can see him rolling his eyes as we head down the steps.

"Ready?" I ask after I've closed the basement door and positioned myself in front of the mirror.

"Yup," Jonah says. "Just tell me when we're done and can play flying crocodile."

I sigh. He really doesn't believe me.

I knock once.

Hisssssss.

Oh! Oh oh OH!

The mirror is hissing, the mirror is hissing!

"Jonah!" I yell. "It's working! Do you hear?"

His eyes are wide open.

"It's hissing!" I knock a second time. A warm light radiates from the mirror. A warm, *purple* light. "See, Jonah?" I turn back to him, and now his jaw is hanging open. He looks like a cartoon of a frog with eyes bulging out of its head. "See?"

"I see!" he says, his voice high-pitched and excited. "It's purple! And hissing! Just like you said!"

Prince barks twice.

"I know!" I exclaim. "Get ready!" I knock a third time and the inside of the mirror starts to spin, faster and faster. Our reflections look as if we got trapped in a washing machine.

"It's spinning!" Jonah squeals.

"Told you so!" I say in a singsong voice. I know I'm gloating, but I've earned it. "Hold my hand and we'll go inside."

"Inside the mirror?" he asks incredulously.

"Yes! We're going into a fairy tale!" I grab his hand. "Ready, Prince?" I ask.

Prince barks again and leaps straight through. Jonah and I follow close behind.

✳ chapter four ✳

Not So Nice to Meet You

Crunch.

We land with a thud on grass and twigs and leaves. Ouch.

I sit up and look around. There are trees everywhere, with pretty orange, red, and yellow leaves. Unlike at home, where it's winter, it must be fall here. It's cool. Not cold, but there's a definite chill in the forest air.

I spot Jonah standing beside a tree. He's not moving.

"Jonah?" I ask. "Are you okay?"

He looks at me and shakes his head.

I jump to my feet. "What's wrong? What happened? Did you hurt yourself?"

He shakes his head again.

"Why aren't you talking, then?"

He opens his mouth and then closes it. Then he opens it again and yells, "ABBY, WHAT IS HAPPENING?"

"We're in a fairy tale," I explain patiently. "I told you. See? There IS a magic mirror in our basement! Next time when I tell you something, you should believe me."

He nods. His eyes are the size of frying pans.

I put my hands on his shoulders. "Did going through spark any memories?"

He doesn't answer.

"Jonah, can you hear me?" I speak directly into his face. "You didn't bang your head on your way in, did you?"

He shakes his head.

"Do you remember anything else?" I ask.

He shakes his head again.

"Crumbs," I say. "Well, hopefully, something here will make you remember."

Jonah twists and chews on his lips. "B-b-but . . . what . . . how . . . *Where* are we?"

"In a fairy tale," I say again. "We just have to figure out which one. Let's see. We're in a forest. That's a clue. But lots of fairy tales take place in forests. Maybe we're in *Hansel and Gretel*?"

Jonah stops chewing his lips and licks them. "Mmm. Is that the one with the house made of candy?"

"Yes, exactly!" Then I shoot him a sharp look. "But, Jonah, if we are in *Hansel and Gretel*, you can't actually eat the house."

"I can't?"

"No. If you eat the house, you'll upset the witch. That's what happened in the original story. Hansel and Gretel upset the witch, and then she tried to cook them. And we always have to try not to mess up the stories."

"How would I mess up a story?" Jonah asks, leaning over to pick up a twig.

I count the ways on my fingers. "If you told Snow White not to eat the poisoned apple, you would mess up the story. If you wore your soccer cleats when you were climbing up Rapunzel's hair, you would mess up the story."

He nods, his eyes still big. "Okay."

Hmm. How do I explain the rest? Fairy tales are complicated. "But sometimes we *want* to mess up the stories. If they have unhappy endings. Like in *The Little Mermaid*. In the movie, she gets married, but in the real story, the Little Mermaid dies!"

Jonah gasps, horrified.

"I know. That's why we changed it. Anyway, we should get moving. What time does your watch say?" I ask.

He looks down at his bare arm. "I'm not wearing my watch."

"What? Why not? I told you, you need to wear your watch whenever we go through the mirror!" Doesn't he listen to anything?

"But . . . but . . . but . . . I didn't believe you!" he cries.

I groan. "Well, then, we have no way of knowing what time it is back home. We have to be back before Mom and Dad get out of bed at seven. If they find our beds empty, they'll have panic attacks. So we can't stay too long here. Just long enough for your memories to come back."

"Ruff, ruff!" Prince runs ahead of us among the trees.

"Wait, Prince! Hold on!" Jonah calls. He starts running after Prince. Then he turns around, and for the first time since we got here, he gives me a smile.

A second later, he trips over a broken tree branch and falls on his flannel butt.

"Jonah, you have to be extra careful here, okay? You don't know what's just around the corner! We don't even know where we are yet!"

"I'm fine," he shouts, popping back up and continuing to run.

I follow him and Prince until we see a gap in the trees.

"Wow," Jonah says.

Wow is right. In front of us is a huge, beautiful, storybook castle. It's made of yellow stone and capped with a blue roof and pointy blue turrets, and it's even surrounded by a moat. The water is sparkling and multicolored, reflecting the autumn leaves around us.

"Hey, Abby?" Jonah calls. "Which fairy tale has a castle in it?"

"A lot of them," I say.

"Does *Jack and the Beanstalk* have a castle?" he asks.

"Yes, but I don't see a beanstalk," I say. Then I laugh. "You always ask about *Jack and the Beanstalk*."

"I do?"

"You do. Maybe we're in *The Princess and the Pea*," I say as all three of us walk across the drawbridge. "That's the one where a princess has to feel a pea under twenty mattresses."

"But how could she feel a pea?" Jonah asks. "Wouldn't it get squished? They should have used a bowling ball."

There's a large silver knocker in the center of the blue door. I lift it and let it bang.

We wait. No one comes to get us.

"Hello?" I call loudly. "Anyone here?"

There's no answer.

"It looks deserted," Jonah says.

Prince barks three times and then runs around the side of the castle.

"Wait, Prince!" I call.

We follow Prince and pass an open window. I peek inside.

It's a big dining room. The table is set with fancy plates and all kinds of food.

I hear a growl next to me, but it's not Prince. It's Jonah's stomach.

"I'm hungry," he says.

"Me too," I say. The food smells amazing. Like fried onions and garlic and cheese.

Jonah licks his lips again. "Do you think it's for us?"

"Why would it be for us?" I ask. "They're not expecting us."

"I don't know how fairy tale land works." He sticks his nose inside. "Maybe they're serving French fries and ketchup."

"Let's keep looking," I say. We wind our way around another bend and suddenly we're in a garden. A rose garden. Great. Just what I want to be reminded of. Roses. Big, blooming, gorgeous red roses.

Prince dashes across the garden.

"Prince! Careful!" I don't want him digging everything up.

"Flowers!" I hear Jonah say behind me. "Perfect!"

Prince lowers his nose and starts sniffing around. He'd better not touch anything.

"This one smells good," Jonah says. "And this one. And this one. Ouch! I just cut my thumb on a thorn!" He sticks his finger in his mouth and sucks on it.

I hear a booming voice behind me. "Where did you come from?"

I spin around.

Standing in front of the garden is . . .

Well . . .

He's . . .

He's at least seven feet tall and hulking. His hands and face are covered in brown fur. He reminds me of a dog. But a human dog. His face is wrinkly, like a pug. He has big, shiny black eyes.

This — creature — is looming ominously over Prince. Oh! He was talking to Prince! He hasn't seen Jonah or me yet!

I motion for Jonah to kneel down next to me and hide behind a rosebush.

"Wh-what is that?" Jonah whispers, his face pale.

"I don't know," I admit. Is it an animal? No. It talked. Animals don't talk. Well, sometimes they do in fairy tale land.

I notice that the thing is wearing black pants. And a buttoned-up white shirt and a black jacket and a purple bow tie. But no shoes. Just furry feet.

Huh?

It comes to me.

It's not a thing.

It's not an animal.

It's half animal, half man.

It's a beast. It's *the* beast.

We're in the story of *Beauty and the Beast*!

✷ chapter five ✷

Here's the Story

W̶e have to save Prince," Jonah whispers. "It's going to eat him!"

"Shhhhh! Stay hidden," I say. "It won't eat him."

"How do you know?" Jonah asks.

"It's not an *it*," I whisper. "It's a *he*. We're in the story of *Beauty and the Beast*."

Jonah looks confused for a second, but then he nods. "Is he Beauty or the beast?"

I giggle and almost fall over. "Seriously? Guess."

He raises an eyebrow. "Beast?"

"Good guess," I say, patting my brother on the head. "And

the beast is not actually that scary in the original story. He's pretty sweet." I peek my head out from behind the shrub. The beast is scratching Prince behind the ears. Aw. I hide again.

"Can you tell me the story?" Jonah asks. "I saw parts of the movie, but I don't remember much."

"You want me to tell you the story right now? We're kind of in the middle of something here."

"Shouldn't I know what's happening?" Jonah asks.

My nana used to read Jonah and me the original fairy tales, which are pretty different from the movies. I listened all the time. Jonah not so much. I peek out once more. The beast and Prince are playing fetch with a gardening shovel. They seem fine. I motion Jonah closer to me.

"Okay. Well, there's a prince. And one day he gets cursed by a fairy." I wiggle my fingers for effect.

"What did he do?"

"The story doesn't say. But it must have been something really, really bad, because the curse is really bad. The fairy turns him into a beast. And he can't turn back into his regular self until someone agrees to marry him just as he is — as a beast. Skip ahead a few years, and a merchant — that's a businessperson — is lost in the forest."

"The forest we just went through?"

"I guess so. Anyway, the merchant comes to the castle and sees a feast laid out."

"Oh! We saw a feast laid out!"

"Not so loud," I say, shooting another glance at the beast and shuddering. Then I feel bad. The beast *seems* nice, but he's still very, very scary looking. "Right. The merchant ate the feast but the beast didn't care. He left the feast for other people. But then the merchant went outside and picked a rose from the garden for his youngest daughter. And when the beast saw him taking the rose, he got *really* mad. He had left all that food for the guy, and then the guy had tried to steal from him. He threatened to kill the merchant!"

Jonah's eyes widen. "Kill? Because he took a rose? Um . . . Abby . . ."

I nod. "I know! That wasn't so nice. But I guess the beast was really protective of his roses or something. Anyway, the merchant begged the beast to spare his life. He told the beast he had three daughters he wanted to live for. The beast told the merchant that he could swap his life for one of his daughters' lives. The merchant had no intention of letting one of his daughters die, but since he wanted to go home and see them again, he agreed to it, thinking he'd buy himself some time. When he got home, his daughter Beauty insisted on honoring the deal and going in his place."

Jonah looks incredulous. "Why would she do that?"

"I have no idea. Maybe she felt guilty because of the rose? Anyway, she moved in with the beast. He thought she was beautiful and loved her right away."

"Did she like him?"

"No. At first, she was horrified by him. He was really nice to her, though. He wanted her to be happy. But he was lonely and a bit grouchy since no one wanted to spend any time with him. But every day that she got to know him better, his looks scared her a little less. He also set her up with her own wing of the castle and filled it with beautiful clothes and jewels. Every night, he would ask her to marry him and she would say no. She still really missed her dad. But then she discovered a magic mirror in her room!"

"Like the one in our basement?"

"Kind of. When Beauty looked inside it, she could see back home. One day, she saw that her dad was sick. She begged the beast to let her go home and promised to return in a week. He agreed. But her sisters were jealous of her and convinced her to stay longer so the beast would get angry. She did stay, and the beast got really sad."

"Aw."

"One night, Beauty dreamt that the beast was dying and she hurried back to his castle. When she got there, she saw that he really *was* dying — he missed her that much. She felt terrible and told him that she would marry him. As soon as she said the words, he turned back into a handsome prince! The end."

"That's nice," Jonah says as I peek back out at the real beast and Prince. They're still playing. "So where are we in the story now?" Jonah asks.

"I don't see Beauty," I whisper, "and the beast is still a beast, so I guess we're near the beginning? Maybe before Beauty's dad the merchant visits?"

"So what do we do? Talk to the beast?"

"Well . . . we don't want to mess up the story, so we have to be careful. But maybe talking to a real live fairy tale character will bring your memories back," I say excitedly. "And then we can use the magic mirror in his castle to go home. I bet we'll just knock and it will slurp us right up."

"You're not afraid to talk to him?" Jonah asks me.

"Not really," I say. "Look how sweet he's being with Prince! He might look like a monster, but he's got a good heart under that thick, gnarled fur."

I take a deep breath and step out from my hiding place. "Excuse me?" I say, my voice a bit shaky. "You must be Beast?"

"Beast probably isn't his real name, Abby," Jonah whispers.

"Oh. Um . . ." My stomach clenches. "What's your real name, sir?"

The beast stands up and makes himself tall. Very tall. He takes five huge steps closer and towers over us.

"You will call me Mr. Beast," he bellows. "Who are you?"

"I'm Abby, and this is my brother, Jonah. That's our dog you're playing with. Isn't he cute?" I squeak.

"Hi," Jonah murmurs.

Mr. Beast keeps glowering at us.

"We're so sorry to have bothered you," I continue, feeling more and more nervous. "You have really nice castle grounds. We didn't mean to interrupt your day. We'll be — we'll be going home soon. If we could just use your magic mi —"

Mr. Beast's lips are pressed together. Hard. His hands are fists. He looks pretty angry. "You're not going anywhere!" he finally yells. "You're a thief!"

My arms start to tremble. "Excuse me? We didn't steal anything!"

"You didn't, but he did!" The beast is pointing right at Jonah. "He stole a rose!"

I turn to Jonah. What is he talking about? And then I look down and notice that on the ground beside Jonah is a single red rose.

Huh? Why is there a plucked rose next to my brother? "Jonah! Did you pick a rose?"

Jonah's cheeks are bright red. Redder than the rose. "I . . . um . . . Yeah. For Mom," he admits. "For her birthday tomorrow. We didn't get her a present!"

He did WHAT? "Jonah! I painted her a picture in art class! I told you it could be from both of us!"

He looks down at the ground. "I saw that. Abby, you're, um, not a very good painter."

Humph.

"Jonah!" I whisper-yell. "You can't come into a fairy tale and steal things! This is exactly what I warned you about!"

Mr. Beast raises an extra-hairy eyebrow.

"But there are so many roses," Jonah says. "I didn't think anyone would notice!"

I turn back to Mr. Beast. "He's really sorry," I say meekly.

"He didn't mean to. The rose is for our mother. It's her birthday tomorrow. I made her a painting already, but apparently it's not good enough for my brother." I grumble the last part.

"I don't care what his excuse is," Mr. Beast yells. "He has no right to take anything in my garden!"

Mr. Beast shoves his giant, hairy finger in Jonah's face.

"You have stolen my rose, little man! Now you must pay."

Pay?

"We didn't bring any money," Jonah says, his voice trembling. He turns to me. "Did we?"

"No, we didn't." And I have a sneaking suspicion Mr. Beast doesn't want money.

"Pay you must," Mr. Beast roars. "WITH YOUR LIFE!"

✳ chapter six ✳

Let's Make a Deal

Whoa! "Hold on there," I say. I wedge my way between Jonah and Mr. Beast. "That's crazy talk!"

"Excuse me?" Mr. Beast hollers.

My mind is racing. This is what happened to Beauty's father! "You can't hurt my brother!"

"Why not?" asks Mr. Beast. He crosses his furry arms. "What will you give me in return?"

"Um . . . ummm . . ." I don't know what to say. I don't even have a watch to trade anymore! I have nothing at all!

Except . . .

I do have something. I have information. "I know how to break your curse!" I announce, my hands on my hips.

Mr. Beast gasps and then narrows his eyes. "You know about the curse?"

I nod. "I do. And I know just the girl who will break it. Promise not to hurt my brother, and I'll prove it to you."

Mr. Beast grazes his fangs against his lower lip. "How do I know you're telling me the truth?"

"I am! I swear!" I hold up my hands. "We know your whole story."

"Jax must have told you," Mr. Beast grumbles. He stomps his foot into the soil. "That purple-haired pipsqueak."

Who's Jax? "It doesn't matter who told me," I say. "What matters is what I know. I know you used to be very handsome before you got cursed."

Mr. Beast furrows his brow. "Thanks, I guess," he says gruffly.

"*And,*" I continue, "I know that a girl named Beauty is supposed to come here. She's beautiful. Just like her name! She'll fall in love with you, and she'll agree to marry you! And then you'll return to your normal, nonbeastly self."

He crosses his hairy, beastly arms. "That's all pretty hard to believe. No one wants to marry me. Trust me."

"It's the truth. I swear." I think fast. "Let us go find this Beauty for you. We'll bring her here and you'll see. She's the love of your life. Your soul mate. The person who ends the curse. Come on, Mr. Beast. What do you have to lose?"

Jonah and I hold our breath.

Mr. Beast closes his eyes for a second. Then he opens them. "All right," he says eventually. "You have until dinner. Or your brother gets hurt."

My heart starts to hammer. Mr. Beast isn't really going to KILL my brother, right? In the story, he doesn't actually kill the merchant, he just threatens to, so I'm sure he won't do it here. He's a nice person underneath all that fur. He really is. He's a big softie. His bark is way worse than his bite. I gulp. Isn't it?

"What time is dinner?" I ask.

"Nine."

Okay. That's a ridiculous hour to eat dinner, but I'm not complaining. I need the time. But it's so late. How does he do it? I'd be starving by then!

"We can do it," I say. What choice do I have? "We'll be back by nine. What time is it now?" I look up. It's a perfect day. It's sunny, but there are a few fluffy clouds in the bright, blue sky.

"Eleven o'clock in the morning."

I nod and motion for my brother and dog to follow me back around to the front of the castle. "Come on, Jonah, Prince, let's go!"

"Noooooooooo." Mr. Beast shakes his head. "Your brother stays here."

Jonah turns white.

My heart stops. "No way," I say.

"Way," Mr. Beast says.

Jonah looks at Mr. Beast and then back at me. "Abby, I'll be okay here."

"No," I cry, grabbing my brother's hand. "The last time I left you alone in a fairy tale, you got turned into a frozen zombie."

His face lights up. "I did? Really?"

"Yes! I can't leave you with someone who just threatened to hurt you." I turn to Mr. Beast. "Take Prince instead. You guys are already friends!"

Prince barks twice.

"No," Mr. Beast says. "How do I know you'll come back for the animal? People don't care about animals."

"I care about my animal!" I protest.

Mr. Beast leans against the stone castle wall. "Clearly not that much if you were willing to trade him for your brother."

Touché.

Jonah steps closer to me and lowers his voice. "Abby, I'll be fine. Mr. Beast is the hero of the story, right? He doesn't actually hurt anyone. He's just trying to scare us to get his way. You saw how sweet he was with Prince. And maybe spending more time with him will make my memories come back."

"But . . . but . . . but . . ." Argh! I guess he's right. And it's not as though I have much of a choice.

I lift my chin and face Mr. Beast. "Do you *promise* not to hurt my brother?"

"I promise not to hurt the boy," Mr. Beast swears, squaring his shoulders. "Just be back in time for dinner."

I swallow hard and squeeze Jonah's hand. He squeezes back, nodding at me reassuringly.

"What will you even do while I'm gone?" I whisper to Jonah.

Jonah shrugs. "I don't know. Do you have a PlayStation, Mr. Beast?" he calls out.

"Huh?" Mr. Beast asks.

"I guess that's a no. What about ketchup? Do you have ketchup?" my brother asks.

"Of course," Mr. Beast huffs. "Homemade ketchup."

Jonah's eyes light up. "Seriously? Yum."

"Are you hungry? I have a lot of food. Mr. and Mrs. Butler!" Mr. Beast calls out, turning toward the castle.

"Oh! I remember that part from the movie!" Jonah says. "Is the housekeeper hiding in a teapot?"

"Excuse me?" Mr. Beast asks incredulously. "Why would anyone hide in a teapot? How could anyone even fit in a teapot?"

An older man and woman walk slowly into the garden. They're both thin, with gray hair and kindly expressions.

"These are my housekeepers," Mr. Beast explains. "Mr. and Mrs. Butler."

They nod and smile at me and Jonah.

"Their name is really Butler?" I ask. Under different circumstances, I'd giggle.

Mr. Beast nods. "Of course. In the kingdom of Kingdom, your name describes you."

"The kingdom of Kingdom?" I ask. "This kingdom is *named* Kingdom?"

"Yes," Mr. Beast says simply.

Oh. Like Beast. And Beauty. That's funny.

"Hello, Mr. and Mrs. Butler!" Mr. Beast says to his servants. "We have a guest!"

"A quest?" says the old man. "Did you say we have a quest? Will we need Pony?"

"Not a quest," Mr. Beast says. "A *guest*."

Mrs. Butler pulls on her earlobe. "Are you tired? Do you need a rest?"

"No," Mr. Beast bellows. "A *guest*! Look!" He points to Jonah.

"Ah!" says Mr. Butler. "Guests! Why didn't you say so, Mr. Beast? We will set up their rooms right away."

"Can I get you something to eat and drink?" asks Mrs. Butler.

"Yes!" says Jonah. "I'm starving. And I heard you have ketchup —"

"Rooms won't be necessary," I cut in. "We're not staying overnight. But I'll be bringing back a girl named Beauty and *she'll* be staying."

"Oh, wonderful," says Mrs. Butler warmly. "I will get three rooms ready. I'll pick out some clothes for you, too! The closets are packed with new outfits I sew in case we ever have visitors!"

I'm about to correct her, but . . . new clothes! Who am I to say no to new clothes?

"Do you have any toys?" Jonah asks.

"Toys?" Mr. Beast snarls. "No."

"I'm sure I can find something to entertain you," Mrs. Butler rushes to say. "We have lots of board games. And tons of books in the basement."

Jonah scowls. "No books, please. I don't like to read. But I'll check out the games. Bye, Abby, you can go, I'll be fine! I'll teach Mr. and Mrs. Butler how to play flying crocodile!"

"Well . . ." I hesitate. I am really torn. I don't want to leave my brother alone. At all. I'm his big sister, his protector. Jonah doesn't remember all the scary things that can happen in fairy tales! And Mr. Beast is pretty scary!

But . . . maybe being here will help Jonah's memories come back. And anyway, I have to find Beauty.

At least Mr. and Mrs. Butler do not seem as if they would let anything bad happen to Jonah.

And since I know Mr. Beast's story, I *do* know that he is good deep down. He didn't hurt the merchant and he didn't hurt Beauty, so he won't hurt my brother. He's not a monster.

It's not like *he* purposely destroyed someone else's painting out of jealousy and then lied about it. Nope.

That was all me.

Maybe fixing up Beauty and Mr. Beast will make up for

what I did. My nana always says that matchmaking is a mitzvah. That means "good deed" in Hebrew.

"Okay," I say. "I'll do it. I'll go. Wait," I add, suddenly panicked. "Where am I going?"

Mr. Beast laughs. "How am I supposed to know? You're the one who said you knew who she was." With that, he turns and marches inside the castle.

He has a point. I try to remember what the story said. The merchant was on his way home when he got lost. So Beauty must live in a nearby town.

"Is there a town nearby?" I ask the servants.

"A crown? You would like a crown?"

"No, a TOWN," I clarify. Although if I'm being honest, I wouldn't mind a crown either.

Mrs. Butler nods. "Yes, it's called Town."

"The town is called Town?" I ask.

She nods again.

Of course it is.

"It's about a two-hour ride," she goes on. "Mr. Beast has never been — he doesn't go out in public — but I go every week to get supplies. I'll give you a map and you can borrow Pony."

I assume Pony is their . . . pony.

At least I'm good with maps. I got all As in our new geography unit in school. And I've had to ride a horse before, and I'm not so bad at it. Now I just have to figure out where in Town Beauty will be. All I know from the original story is that she likes books. "Is there a bookstore in Town?" I ask. "Or a library?"

Mrs. Butler shakes her head. "No," she says. "But if you go to Main Street, you can ask around to see if anyone knows her."

I nod. "Okay. I'll go."

I give Jonah a long, tight hug. "Be careful," I whisper to him. "Be safe."

"I will," Jonah assures me, hugging me back. Then he steps out of my embrace and waves to me. "Good luck! Oh, and take Prince. He can help you find her."

I nod again. Prince *is* good at finding stuff. Last week, he found the TV remote, which had somehow ended up under my parents' bed.

Although Prince was probably the one who put it there. Anyway.

Time to go to Town.

✳ chapter seven ✳

It's a Beauty-ful Day in the Neighborhood

I climb onto Pony's back, Prince in my lap.

For a pony, Pony is pretty big. But he's also adorable.

I spread out the map and take a look.

Okay. This doesn't seem that hard. I have to take Rocky Path to Winding Path to Straight Road to Highway to Boulevard to Main Street.

"Giddyup!" I say, which seems to work, because Pony moves, bumping down Rocky Path.

I bounce a bit from side to side. Prince grabs my leg with his paws.

I start to worry. Did I really just leave my brother alone with a beast? A beast who threatened to kill him? Am I seriously riding a pony into a forest I've never been in before? That does not seem very smart of me.

"I don't know if this was my best decision," I tell Prince and Pony.

Prince barks. Pony whinnies.

We continue trotting down Rocky Path.

"Not smart at all," I add. "It's not totally my fault, though, is it? I barely had time to think my decision through."

They bark and whinny again.

"I know what you guys are thinking," I say. "What if we can't find Beauty? Or what if, when we do find her, she doesn't want to come with us?"

Prince barks twice. I guess that means yes. Pony neighs. Obviously, they both agree with me.

Yep. I'm going to pretend Prince, Pony, and I are having a discussion, and that's that.

"What should I say to her to convince her to come to Mr. Beast's castle?"

"Neigh!"

"No, Pony," I say. "I can't just tell her the truth. Wait, Pony, turn here by that waterfall. It's Winding Path."

Pony turns and I pat him on the back. "Good job. Where was I? Oh, right. I can't tell her that Mr. Beast is actually a gorgeous prince, because then she can't break the curse. The curse has to be broken by someone who doesn't know what he really looks like."

Two barks.

"True, Prince, we can beg her to come with us. We can tell her that the beast is keeping my brother hostage and maybe she would want to help. She was willing to help her father in the original story, right? But that was her father! We're not her family. She doesn't even know us. Would you trade yourself for a hostage that you don't even know?"

"*Neigh.*"

"No, me neither." I think back to art class. "But we already know I'm a monster, so we can't judge her on what *I* would do."

"*Ruff!*"

"I am too a monster. I ruined Penny's painting on purpose. I'm the worst. But let's get back to the problem. How do we convince Beauty to save Jonah?"

"*Growl!*"

"True, Jonah is just a kid and Beauty might feel bad. But she might not. We need some other ideas."

"*Neigh!*"

"Pony! That's not very nice. You think we should trick her? Well, I guess we could. I'm glad you thought of it and not me. But yes, desperate times call for desperate measures. And the ends might justify the means. Oh! I have an idea! We could tell her that there's a ball! And that she's invited! And she'll come with us back here, and then I'll take Jonah and run! She'll be angry, of course, but after all is said and done, she'll get her happy ending and she'll get over it. Right?"

"Grunt. Neigh. Snort. Ruff."

"Okay, then never mind."

About two hours later, we turn on to Main Street. It looks exactly how I imagined a Main Street would look. It's a pretty, cobblestoned street lined with all kinds of stores. There's a grocery store called Supermarket. A clothing store called Boutique. Oooh, there's even a store called Cheese Shop.

My stomach growls. I could so eat some cheese right now.

Stay focused, I tell myself. I will just go into Cheese Shop to ask for directions.

I leave Pony outside and carry Prince. When I push open the door, a little bell rings.

Mmmm, it smells so good in here. I wonder if they have cheese sticks. Maybe they're giving away samples.

"Well, hello there!" the girl behind the counter says. She looks just a little older than a teenager. She's pretty, with blond spiky hair and lots of freckles. She's wearing a white apron that says CHEESE SHOP.

She lowers her face to Prince's eye level. "Aren't you a handsome little guy?" she asks him. "Would you like a special treat? I make special animal cheeses," she tells me. "Okay with you?"

"Sure," I say.

She puts a plate down on the floor in front of Prince.

To say Prince likes the cheeses is to put it mildly. He devours them. His tail wags all over the place.

"What can I get for you?" the girl asks me. "You look hungry."

"Oh, um, thanks, but I don't have any money on me."

"Well, you're in luck," the girl says. "I was just testing out a new sandwich. Grilled apple and cheese on a bun. Want to try one? My treat. You'll have to be honest and tell me if you like it."

"Yes, please!" I say, and devour half of it in three bites. Mmmm. "Thank you. It's amazing."

"Hurrah," she says, beaming. "Now, if you didn't come in for cheese, why *did* you come in?"

I lick a stray piece of melted cheddar off my fingers. "I'm

looking for someone. She's about sixteen or so. I think her name might be Beauty? Do you know her?"

The girl smiles. "Beauty! Of course I know Beauty! She's . . . well, she's beautiful! She has the most amazing hair. And skin. Invisible pores. And she's such a *good* person," the girl goes on. "Always doing things for other people. She was a few years behind me at school. I was in her older sister's class."

"Great," I cheer. "Do you know where I can find her?"

"Not too far. She lives in a cottage about an hour outside of town."

"Oh," I say. Another hour of riding Pony? At least I have some strength after eating.

"But you know what?" the girl adds. "I bet you can find her at Soup Kitchen. She volunteers there at least twice a week. Or maybe she'll be at Orphanage. She reads to the children every morning. Or maybe at Garbage Dump? She helps with the recycling."

"Wow, she does a lot of good stuff," I say. I can't help but feel jealous. Beauty sounds like the type of person who would never ruin someone else's painting.

So now I'm jealous of someone because they're nice? What is wrong with me?

I *am* a green-eyed monster. I am more monsterlike than Mr. Beast!

The girl nods. "She does do a lot of good stuff. She's really beautiful inside and out."

"She sounds amazing," I say. I should really do more volunteer work. Maybe I should have a bake sale. Or a car wash. I want to read to orphans. Where can I find orphans?

"Oh, look! There she is now!" The girl points out the window. "She's helping Grumpy Great-Grandma with her groceries!"

"Someone's name is Grumpy Great-Grandma?" I ask.

"Yup." She shakes her head. "She is very, very grumpy."

I laugh. "What's your name?" I ask.

"Freckles," the girl says with a smile.

I spin around to face the window and immediately spot Beauty. How could I miss her? She is, indeed, gorgeous. She has long black curly hair and big brown eyes, and she is wearing a white dress that perfectly shows off her dark brown skin.

I'm not the only one who notices her. Every man, woman, and child on the street has stopped moving to stare at her. She's like a movie star.

Not that she notices. Beauty is carrying six grocery bags, and a very old woman is holding on to her arm. This woman looks old enough to be Mr. or Mrs. Butler's grandmother. She's hunched over and using a cane.

Seeing Beauty's helpfulness in action makes my heart lift. Maybe she will want to help Jonah!

"Prince! Let's go," I holler, stuffing the rest of my sandwich in my mouth. I try to tell Freckles, "Thank you so much," but because my mouth is full, it ends up coming out as "Tank ew oh mut."

Freckles smiles, and I wave and run outside.

"Be careful!" Grumpy Great-Grandma yells at Beauty. "Carry the bags higher!"

"Sorry, Grumpy Great-Grandma," Beauty says. She lifts the bags higher.

"Now they're swinging!" Grumpy Great-Grandma shrieks. "Are you trying to bang up the bananas?"

Grumpy Great-Grandma really is very, very grumpy.

Beauty looks at me and smiles. She has two perfect dimples. She also has perfect, white shiny teeth.

"Hello," I say. "Beauty?"

"Hello," she says. "Can I help you?"

"Actually, that would be great," I say.

"Less talking, more walking," says Grumpy Great-Grandma.

"Sorry, Grumpy Great-Grandma," Beauty says. Then she turns to me. "It's not her fault. She has a bad hip."

"No problem," I say, walking along beside them. Prince trots behind us.

How to begin? It seems strange to just come out and ask someone if she wouldn't mind going to live with a beast so you could have your brother back.

Grumpy Great-Grandma narrows her eyes at me. "If you want to talk to Beauty, you should at least give her a hand and carry one of my bags."

"Of course," I say. "Sorry! Let me help." I take two bags from Beauty and clear my throat. "So. My name is Abby, and my brother's name is Jonah. And Jonah is why I need help."

"Abby? And Jonah?" Beauty says with wide eyes. "Wow. I've never heard those names before! So original!"

I almost laugh. "Thank you. Well, see, we stopped by a palace owned by a guy named Mr. Beast. Have you ever heard of him?"

She shakes her head. "No," she says.

I need to continue this story carefully. I can't let it slip that Mr. Beast is secretly a handsome prince. That would mess everything up. "We stopped at the palace and met Mr. Beast. But my brother picked one of the flowers, and Mr. Beast . . ." I debate whether I should tell her that he threatened to kill my brother. Probably not. No need to scare her unnecessarily. "Mr. Beast insisted on keeping Jonah. But he can't keep Jonah, you see. We don't live anywhere near here. We have to get home. And he's only seven! Mr. Beast said we could trade Jonah if we could find someone else who was willing to stay there. He lives in an amazing castle. It's gorgeous." I pause. Now I have to ask her if she'll trade places with him. But how can I ask her that? It's a crazy thing to ask. But I have to. I have to just do it. "So . . ." I begin.

"Okay," she says suddenly.

"Okay what?"

She nods. "Okay, I'll take your brother's place."

Huh. "You will? But I didn't even ask you to!"

"I know. But you were going to, weren't you?"

"I was! I was going to beg!"

She smiles as we reach Grumpy Great-Grandma's stoop. "You don't need to beg. You need help. And I volunteer."

As pleased as I am that Beauty is so willing to take his place, I'm kind of shocked. Why is she so willing? She doesn't even know Jonah. She doesn't even know *me*!

"Let's go!" Beauty says, putting the bags down by the door.

"You're not going anywhere before you finish putting away my bananas," Grumpy Great-Grandma orders.

I peer inside the bags. All I see are bananas. "You didn't buy anything else?" I ask.

Beauty lowers her voice. "Bananas are all she eats. For breakfast, lunch, and dinner. Let's drop these off and then we'll go save Jordan, 'kay?"

"Er, Jonah," I say.

She smiles. "Right. Jonah!"

After we drop off the bananas, we return to Pony, who's still waiting outside Cheese Shop.

"Pony is pretty strong. He can take both of us," I explain to Beauty. "Will you just hold Prince?"

"You know a prince?" Beauty looks around in wonder.

"Oh. Um. Prince is my dog," I explain, gesturing to him. He barks. I don't mention that *Mr. Beast* is an actual prince in case that messes up the curse.

"Ah. I see." Beauty bends down, scooping up Prince.

"Do I need to stop at my house to pick up clothes?" Beauty asks as we all get on Pony.

"I don't think so," I say. "They have tons of clothes at the palace."

I don't want Beauty to stop at her house in case her family talks her out of coming. But that's selfish of me, isn't it? If she wants to say good-bye to her family, I shouldn't get in the way of that.

"But we can stop at your place if you want to," I add.

She hesitates. "My dad just left on a business trip last week. And my sisters . . ." Her voice trails off. "My sisters don't really like me."

"How come?" I ask.

"I don't know," she admits. "No matter what I do, they get annoyed. I try so hard to be nice, but I can tell they don't really want me at home."

I remember what the original story said. Beauty's sisters are infected with the green-eyed monster. They're jealous of Beauty. Which I kind of understand. Beauty is pretty perfect.

"So maybe staying at Mr. Beast's castle for a bit isn't a terrible thing," Beauty goes on. "How long will I be there, do you think?"

"Well, um . . ." *Cough, cough. Forever?* "Not too long," I say instead.

Beauty sits up straight. "Okay, then. Take me to Mr. Beast's."

∗ chapter eight ∗

Change of Plans

As we trot back toward Mr. Beast's palace, I can't believe how well everything is working out. It's still late afternoon and I've already found Beauty and gotten her to agree to trade places with Jonah. In a few minutes, we'll be at the castle. I'll drop off Beauty, and Jonah and I will be able to go home through the castle's magic mirror. Easy peasy! I bounce in my saddle. Maybe my brother's memories came back, too!

But I shouldn't get ahead of myself. First I'll introduce Beauty to Mr. Beast and let the story unfold. It will be sweet to watch them fall in love and see Mr. Beast's curse reversed.

I look behind me at Beauty. Hopefully, she won't freak out

when she meets the beast. I didn't really give her much information about him. Maybe I should warn her about what he looks like? Yes. I definitely should.

"Um, Beauty," I begin, "about Mr. Beast . . ."

"Yes?" she asks.

"Well, he's called Mr. Beast for a reason."

"Is it because he's hairy? My grandfather was very hairy. That was his name actually. Hairy."

"Well, Mr. Beast *is* hairy. But that's only part of it. See, he looks like . . . a beast."

She cocks her head to the side. "How so?"

I gulp. "He's scary-looking. Not like a monster, but . . ." I clear my throat. "Well, kind of like a monster."

"Oh!" Beauty pulls a curl tightly around her finger. Then she lifts her chin. "That doesn't change anything. I said I would switch places with your brother and I will. I don't go back on my word."

"Okay," I say, heaving a sigh of relief. "I just wanted to warn you."

We trot for a few more minutes until we turn onto Rocky Path.

She points up ahead. "Is that the castle?"

"Yup. Pretty, huh? I hope you like it. Thank you for coming!"

"I'm happy to help," she says. "I'm always happy to help."

Pony stops before the moat, and Beauty and I dismount. "Follow me!" I say brightly, taking Prince from Beauty. I am trying to keep my voice extra light and fluffy so Beauty still thinks she's walking into a great situation.

We cross the drawbridge, and I knock on the front door. "Hello!" I call. "It's Abby. I'm back! Before dinnertime. And I brought the girl I was telling you about! Beauty!"

Mrs. Butler opens the door.

"Hello," I say serenely. "We'd like to talk to Mr. Beast."

She holds a hand to her ear. "You'd like to have a feast?"

"No, no, no," I say. "I'd like to talk to Mr. Beast. Although I'm not opposed to a feast if you have one ready. But Mr. Beast is more important."

"Speak up, deary!" she says, pointing to her ear.

"Mr. Beast, please!" I yell.

"Oh, one second," she says before turning and bustling away.

I wait anxiously, chewing my nails. I hope Jonah is okay.

"You're back," Mr. Beast booms a second later, stepping into the doorway.

Beauty gasps.

I shoot her a look. That's exactly why I warned her! So she wouldn't gasp!

I grab Beauty's hand and squeeze it *hard*.

"Hi, Mr. Beast," I say. "This is Beauty. She volunteered to stay here instead of Jonah. Right, Beauty?"

Beauty nods even though her eyes are popping out of her head.

"Yes," Beauty squeaks. "I've come to switch places with Jason —"

"Jonah," I correct.

"Jonah," she says.

Mr. Beast studies Beauty with narrowed eyes. Then he sighs.

"I changed my mind," he says with a shake of his head.

"Excuse me?" I ask. What does that mean, he changed his mind? I must have heard wrong. Am I becoming like the Butlers?

"I changed my mind," he repeats. "I know I told you Beauty could trade places with Jonah. But I'd rather keep Jonah." He nods. "Yeah. Jonah stays."

I don't understand.

"Huh?" says Beauty.

"Jonah stays. I don't want Beauty."

"But I'm here to help," Beauty says.

"I don't want your help," Mr. Beast snaps.

"You can't do this!" I exclaim.

"I can, too," he says.

"I have to take my brother home to Smithville," I say, starting to panic. "You're not allowed to keep him."

"You can't stop me," he barks. "I make the rules."

This can't be happening! Mr. Beast needs to fall in love and get engaged or his curse will last forever!

"Can we speak in private, please?" I hiss.

"No," he says. "We have nothing left to talk about."

"But . . . but . . ." I have to talk to Mr. Beast, but I can't risk Beauty hearing what I need to say. "Um, Beauty, would you mind blocking your ears?"

She shrugs and sticks her fingers in her ears.

"Beast — sorry — *Mr.* Beast, the curse says that someone who doesn't know who you really are has to accept your marriage proposal so you can change back!"

"I know," Mr. Beast says. He looks down at his feet. "But Jonah is like the kid brother I always wanted! We've been having a good time playing games. I'd rather do that than have to convince some unsuspecting girl to fall in love with me. I've tried it before, and it never works. I'm done trying. Jonah's my friend. And he doesn't make me feel bad about myself. I'm not trading him for some girl who will. Jonah stays. Beauty goes."

Behind Mr. Beast, I see a figure in the hallway. It's my brother!

"Jonah!" I cry out. "Do you hear what's happening? He's going back on his deal! This can't happen. We have to do something! Run, Jonah, run!"

Jonah ambles over to the door and stares at me quizzically. "I'm not running," he says. "Why would I run? This place is amazing!"

I gaze at him in shock. "What?"

"You were right, Abby — fairy tales are the best!"

"B-but we have to go home!"

"No way! I'm having the best time! I'm in a castle! I taught Mr. Beast how to play flying crocodile!"

He's got to be kidding me. "You can play flying crocodile at home!"

"Mom and Dad don't let me play at home! They make me read! Mr. Beast doesn't care if I read. And he has the best snacks. Ketchup-flavored chips! Have you ever heard of such a thing? They're delicious."

"But . . . but . . ."

Mr. Beast shrugs. "Sorry, but as you can see, your brother wants to stay."

And with that, Mr. Beast slams the door in my face.

✳ chapter nine ✳

Kink in the Plan

$g$reat, just great. What am I supposed to do now? Obviously, Jonah can't stay here forever. That's insane. As if I could go home to Smithville without him!

Sorry, Mom and Dad, but Jonah moved into a palace to live with a beast. I tried to bring him home, but he just doesn't want to practice his reading. Happy birthday, Mom!

Ridiculous. Absolutely ridiculous. What is wrong with my brother?

I turn back to see Beauty, who seems equally upset. Her lower lip is quivering. "Abby, why didn't Mr. Beast want me to stay? Did he not like me? Does he not think I'm beautiful on the inside? I really want to be beautiful on the inside! I try really hard!"

"It's not you," I say. "It's him. He doesn't even know you."

"But he looked at me! He saw me! He must think I'm ugly or a horrible person or something."

"No," I say. "There's no way he thought you were ugly. And I'm sure he doesn't think you're a horrible person. It sounds like he's had his heart broken before and he doesn't want it to happen again. I think he's just protecting himself."

I walk up and down the drawbridge, trying to think. I need a plan. A really good one. I need to change Mr. Beast's mind. What will change his mind? What can I do to get him to send Jonah home?

Hmm. He needs to fall in love with Beauty.

Yes. That's exactly it. If he falls in love with Beauty, then he'll *want* her to stay.

I thought I'd have to convince *Beauty* to give Mr. Beast a chance. But instead, I have to convince Mr. Beast to give Beauty a chance!

I bet it won't even be that hard. He fell in love with her in the original story, didn't he? And he would have fallen in love with her if Jonah and I hadn't shown up. So it will happen eventually. It has to.

She's Beauty and he's the Beast. They're the title of the story! They're made to be together. They're like ketchup and French fries. They're going to fall in love for sure.

Okay, sometimes in the other stories, the characters got new happy endings, but the Cinderella story wasn't called *Cinderella and the Prince*, now, was it? No, it was not.

"He's going to like you," I tell Beauty. "I promise."

"But how?" Beauty asks. "He locked us outside!"

Good point. I knock on the door again.

"Go away!" Mr. Beast yells. "Your brother is happy here!"

"Exactly," I yell back. "*My* brother! Not yours!" I take a deep breath. "But I'll make you a deal, Mr. Beast!"

Beast opens the door a crack. "What's the deal?"

"Jonah can stay," I say. "For a bit. But not without us."

He looks confused. "You *want* to stay here?"

I nod. "I can't leave Jonah alone. He's my little brother. It's my responsibility to watch him. I shouldn't have left him alone before, but I didn't have a choice. No way am I leaving him again. I'm sure you have enough rooms. This place looks huge."

"Of course I have enough rooms," he says gruffly. "But no one has ever asked to stay here before. No one has *willingly* wanted to spend time with me. I pay Mr. and Mrs. Butler to be here."

"You can't be that bad," I say.

I hear my brother shout, "Wahoo!" from the other room.

"Jonah seems to be having a fun time," I add.

Mr. Beast smiles and I can see his fangs. "He *is* having a fun time. But most people are scared of me."

I straighten my shoulders. "Well, I want to stay! And Beauty does, too. And Prince."

Mr. Beast bends down and motions to Prince. "Hello, little dog. Do you want to play? Come play!"

Prince leaps onto Mr. Beast and licks his face.

Mr. Beast laughs. It's actually a nice-sounding laugh, not scary at all. Then he turns around and goes back into the palace. He leaves the door open behind him.

"He won't even look at me," Beauty whispers. "Maybe I should leave."

"No," I say. "Please, Beauty. You need to get Mr. Beast to like you. Just be your awesome self."

She hesitates. "Okay," she says, and follows me inside.

The foyer is all white marble. There are chandeliers everywhere, too. It's very castle-like.

In front of me I see the dining room that I spied earlier. To my right I hear laughter. I follow the sound until I spot Jonah and Mr. Beast playing a card game. Mr. Beast is sitting on a brown couch, and Jonah is sitting on a small chair opposite him.

Jonah waves. "You have to play this, Abby! It's so much fun. It's called trump. Whoever has the highest card wins! Mr. B taught it to me."

"Great," I say, and step inside.

Now how am I going to get Mr. Beast and Beauty to fall in love?

I think back to the original story. How did they fall in love?

Hmm. Technically Beauty only fell in love with him when she thought he was dying.

But let's forget that part.

They spent a lot of time together. Which means they got to know each other.

Okay. We can do that.

"Beauty," I say. "Why don't you sit down on the couch?"

She nods and takes a seat beside Mr. Beast. She fans her white dress out around herself.

"Hello," she says to him. "I'm Beauty."

"Hello, Beauty," he says without looking up from his cards.

I need Mr. Beast and Beauty to chat without Jonah and me distracting them.

"Jonah, can I talk to you alone?" I ask.

"Now?" he sputters. "I'm in the middle of a game!"

"You can play after," I snap. "It's urgent."

Jonah sighs. "Okay, okay. Be right back, Mr. B," he says, and follows me out into the marble foyer. "What's up?" he asks.

First I throw my arms around him. "Are you okay?"

"I'm great. I'm having fun! Mr. B is the best."

"Have any of your memories come back?"

He shakes his head. "No. But we haven't been here that long. I bet they will."

"You know you can't stay here forever, right?"

He shrugs. "I know. I wasn't going to stay here forever. Just a week or so. Like a vacation?"

"Jonah, we can't stay here for a week! We have no idea how long that is at home! You know how time is different in every fairy tale."

He stomps his foot. "I *don't* know, actually! I don't remember the other fairy tales! I wish I did but I don't! This is all I know! And I don't want to go home yet. It's not a big deal!"

"Jonah, it *is* a big deal! Now Mr. Beast doesn't want Beauty to stay. You messed up the story!"

He twists his lower lip. "I did? But how?"

"By being so much fun to hang out with!"

His makes a quizzical face. "Huh?"

"You were so much fun that Mr. Beast doesn't want you to go. He wants you to be his little brother," I say. My voice sounds a bit bitter. Jonah is *my* little brother. *Mine.* My head hurts and I rub my temples with my fingers.

"Oops," Jonah says. "It's not my fault I'm so much fun to be around. And it's not my fault you kept knocking on the mirror night after night!"

"I did that because going into fairy tales is fun! And because I wanted your memories to come back. Not because I wanted you to move in with Mr. Beast and mess up the story."

"But you said we mess the stories up all the time, right? Can't we just fix it?"

"Yes, Jonah, but it's not so easy. We have no control over what's going to happen. We could get hurt."

BANG!

Jonah and I jump.

"Sorry!" we hear Mr. Butler yell from the kitchen. "Just putting dishes away!"

"It's okay!" I call back. Then I look back at Jonah. "Come on," I say to him. "You know we can't stay."

"All right," he says with a sigh, putting his hands in his pockets. "What should we do, then?"

"We have to get Beauty and Mr. Beast to fall in love. That's why I wanted them to be alone. Peek inside and see if they're in love yet, will ya?"

Jonah peeks inside.

"I don't think they're in love yet," he says.

"How can you tell?"

"Look for yourself."

I look in.

Mr. Beast and Beauty are sitting on opposite ends of the couch.

They are not talking. At all. She is looking at the window and he is looking in the opposite direction at a potted plant.

Clearly, they will need some more help falling in love. *Lots* of help.

✶ chapter ten ✶

Mirror, Mirror

I watch forlornly as Mr. Beast stands up from the couch and
excuses himself. "I will see you all at nine o'clock for dinner,"
he says before leaving.

Beauty sighs.

Jonah and I exchange a defeated look.

Mrs. Butler appears and shows the three of us up a grand
staircase and down a long hallway. "This is the guest wing,"
she says.

"A wing?" Jonah exclaims. "We get a whole wing?"

"Yes, Jonah," I say. "A whole wing." It's not the first time
we've gotten a wing in a fairy tale. I'm excited to get to the room,

though. I want to get settled so we can focus on making a plan. A plan that involves a list. I like lists.

Our wing consists of a pretty sitting area that leads into three huge square bedrooms and one large marble bathroom with an extra-large soaking tub.

Beauty goes into her room and looks out the window. "It's very pretty. But we really are in the middle of nowhere. We're even more in the middle of nowhere than my dad's cottage." She yawns. "Sorry. I've been up since five A.M."

"How come?" I ask.

"Breakfast shift at Soup Kitchen," she explains.

"Why don't you take a nap?" I ask.

"A nap? I never have time to nap. After the breakfast shift, I have to go to Garbage Dump to help with the recycling."

"You have time now," I say.

She nods, looking pleased. "Okay. I will. Good suggestion."

I close her door and then follow Jonah into his room.

"This is amazing!" he squeals, springing onto his super-high canopy bed.

The carpet is extra soft, the wallpaper has a pretty flower pattern, and the drapes are shimmery silver. "It *is* nice," I admit.

"Does it bring back any other castle memories? Like the time we visited *The Little Mermaid*?"

"Nope!" Jonah says and then jumps up and down on his bed.

I walk out into the sitting area. It has two plush suede couches, a leather chair, and a shiny wooden desk. On one of the walls is a huge silver mirror. On another, there's a large gold clock.

"It's five thirty here," I say worriedly. "I just wish I knew what time it was back home. Mom and Dad could already be awake and looking for us. They could have called the police again!"

"They called the police?" Jonah asks, following me into the sitting room. He stands on one of the couch cushions and leaps off.

"Yes, once before," I say. I twist my hands together. "I really hope they're not awake."

"I'm pretty sure they're still asleep," Jonah says, climbing back onto the couch.

"You have no way of knowing that," I say.

"Yeah, I do."

"No, you don't," I argue.

"Yes, I do. Look." Jonah points to the silver mirror on the wall.

"Oh my gosh!" I yell and jump back.

My parents are IN the mirror.

Not like trapped inside. I can actually see them in the mirror. It's as if there's a camera on their ceiling and I can see them in their beds, all the way in Smithville. They are both fast asleep.

"*SNORTSH*," snores my dad. Except it's more like "*SNOOOOOOOOORTSH*" in slow motion. Usually, time at home is slower than time in fairy tales. So maybe a minute at home is an hour here. Which means that this snore could go on for hours.

"This must be the magic mirror!" I exclaim. Then I add in a whisper, "Do you think they can hear us?"

"CAN YOU HEAR US?" Jonah hollers at the top of his lungs.

"Jonah! Shush! Do you want to wake them up?"

"I don't think they can hear us," Jonah says. "I think it's a one-way mirror. Like at the police station."

"When have you ever been to a police station?" I ask.

"I haven't," he says. "Unfortunately. But I've watched TV, and a lot of shows take place in a police station."

"Okay." I let out a sigh of relief. "This is helpful. We know they're still sleeping. We don't know what time it is, but we know they're not awake and looking for us."

"We *do* know what time it is," Jonah says. "Look at their alarm clock."

Oh! He's right! The clock says it's one thirty A.M. Let's see. We arrived in Kingdom around ten in the morning, which was midnight at home. An hour and a half has gone by there, and seven and a half hours here. "That means time is going about five times slower there," I say, calculating. "For every hour at home, it's five hours here. And since they get up around seven, that gives us about twenty-seven and a half hours to make things right."

"You're really good at math," Jonah says.

"Thanks," I say. If only I were half as good at painting.

"That seems like a lot of hours," Jonah adds.

"Time flies when you're having fun," I say. "Also when you're messing up fairy tales. But we are one step ahead anyway. We know how to get home."

"Yeah!" He scratches his head. "How do we get home?"

"I told you," I say. "We knock on this magic mirror."

Jonah nods. "That makes sense. We're not going to end up in their room, are we?"

"I don't think so. We always end up back in the basement. Anyway. Now all we need to figure out is how to get Mr. Beast and Beauty to fall in love," I say. "And then we can leave."

"Or we could just leave now. Knock on the mirror and go," Jonah says.

"Oh!" He's right. We *could* just go home. But what if Mr. Beast tells Beauty to leave? Or what if she takes off? Then they'll never fall in love and their lives will be ruined. "No," I argue, "we have to stay and make sure the story happens like it's supposed to. Mom and Dad are sleeping anyway."

"Good point," says Jonah. "So what's our plan?"

I've been thinking about this. "We should have them go on dates."

"Dates?" Jonah frowns. "Like grown-ups do?"

"Yeah!" I say. "Let's make a list of dates for Beauty and Mr. Beast to go on!"

I spot a paper and pen on the desk, make myself comfy in the leather chair, and write:

DATES FOR BEAUTY AND MR. BEAST

Hmm. I tap my pen against the table. "What kind of dates do Mom and Dad go on when they go out on Saturday nights?

Jonah hangs upside down off the couch. "They go to Trattoria for dinner."

"Right," I say. "Okay! We can do that. Beauty and Mr. Beast will have dinner together. A romantic dinner! Tonight! We're having dinner soon anyway. We'll just make it romantic."

I write:

1. Romantic dinner

"But we're going to be there, too," Jonah says, still upside down. "Don't they have to be alone for it to be romantic?"

"Yes," I say. "Maybe we'll tell them nine is too late for us to eat, and we need to go to sleep. It *is* really late, and we are just kids."

"But I'm hungry!"

My stomach rumbles. So am I. "How about we eat a little and then excuse ourselves before dessert?"

"But I like dessert," Jonah protests, his face turning red from being upside down.

"Jonah! You can have dessert at home!"

"Fine," he grumbles.

"What else do Mom and Dad do for date nights?" I ask.

"They go to the movies," Jonah says.

"Perfect." I write:

2. Go to the movies

"Although," I say, picturing the quaint, old-fashioned town. "I don't think there are any movie theaters in the kingdom of Kingdom."

"Could they watch something on Netflix?" Jonah suggests. He's moved over to the other couch and is now lying upside down off that one.

I sputter. "Jonah! There's no Netflix here!" I scratch out "*2. Go to the movies*" and suddenly have a brilliant idea. "But! We could *make* a movie! I mean, we can put on a show for them."

I write:

2. Go to a show

"Oh, cool!" Jonah cries, flipping right side up. "We could put on a play. Or sing a song for them. Or do a dance routine for them!"

I don't want to hurt his feelings, but Jonah doesn't have the best singing voice. Or acting skills. Or dance abilities. Maybe a show isn't the best idea. Hmm.

"Or instead of the two of us putting *on* a play, maybe the two of them could *play* a game. The game you guys were just playing, maybe?"

"Flying crocodile?" Jonah asks hopefully.

"No. The card game."

"Trump!" He somersaults off the couch and sprawls across the floor.

"Yes."

"Good idea," Jonah says. "Mom and Dad play rummy sometimes on vacation. It'll be like that." He climbs back on the couch and starts jumping.

"Careful," I say. "One of these days, you're going to hurt yourself. But yes. Like rummy. Exactly."

I cross out "*2. Go to a show*" and write:

2. Play trump

"So no singing or dancing?" Jonah asks.

"No," I say. But then I have a flash of remembering Mom and Dad dancing at a wedding. "But *they* can dance. Beauty and Mr. Beast dance in the movie! Dancing is really romantic. Don't you remember Nana saying that she fell in love with Grandpa after they danced together at a school social for the first time?"

"Oh, yeah!" Jonah says.

I add:

3. Dance together

I relax against the back of the chair. "Perfect. These are three great date ideas. If they do what I say, Beauty and Mr. Beast are going to fall in love for sure."

Jonah somersaults off the couch again and bangs into the wall. "Ouch," he says, rubbing his elbow.

Now if only *Jonah* would do what I say, we'd be all set.

* chapter eleven *

Let's Eat

he dinner bell chimes at nine o'clock. My stomach is rumbling like a volcano.

After Jonah and I finished making our list of date ideas, we went back to our rooms to change out of our pj's. There were tons of clothes in my closet! Including a beautiful purple satin gown and a silver tiara. And at least ten pairs of super-cute pajamas. Does Mr. Beast think we're staying that long? He didn't even want us here in the first place! Is he really planning on keeping us forever? Doesn't he realize we can sneak back home through the mirror at any time?

I change into a green-and-white polka-dot dress and green shoes, then stop by Jonah's room. First, though, I peek into the magic mirror in the sitting room to make sure my parents are still in sleepyland. Yup, they are. Hurrah!

Jonah is wearing a new pair of gray pants, a crisp white shirt, and black suspenders. Except the suspenders are all tangled and crossed on his front instead of his back. He looks pretty proud of himself, so I decide not to fix them.

"You look very handsome," I say.

He preens. "Thank you. I had to change. My pajamas had ketchup all over them."

I laugh. "I'm surprised you didn't try to eat them."

When we get to the dining room, Mr. Beast is sitting at the head of the table. It's a very long table. Like, ridiculously long. Like you could sit ten people on each side. But instead, it's set for just five people. Mr. Beast, Beauty, me, Jonah, and . . .

Prince jumps onto one of the seats.

"No, Prince, not at the table," I say.

"Why shouldn't he sit at the table?" Mr. Beast huffs. "Is he not good enough to sit at the table because he's covered in fur?"

"Oh," I say. "I guess he can sit at the table." Oops.

Beauty finally comes down a few minutes later and says, "Hi, everyone."

Beauty looks, of course, beautiful in a new red dress. It brings out the warmth in her skin and shows off her glossy, curly black hair.

Unfortunately, Mr. Beast barely looks at or acknowledges her.

"Hello!" says Mrs. Butler, appearing with food on a tray. "We will start off with goat cheese soup. Then we will be serving ricotta ravioli. And for dessert, we will have chocolate cheesecake. Doesn't that sound delicious?"

We all nod. It really does.

I scoop up my soup with my spoon. Mmm. I wish I could have this at home. I wish I had a Mrs. Butler at home, too.

There is even a special plate of dog food for Prince, which he happily inhales.

"The meal is delicious," I tell Mrs. Butler.

"No, no, dear, you don't need to help with the dishes. I'll do them."

I giggle. "No, Mrs. Butler, I said the meal is *delicious*. You're a wonderful cook. But I *am* happy to help with the dishes!"

Now she laughs. "Cook? I don't cook! Mr. Beast is the cook!"

Mr. Beast flushes.

"He is?" I ask. "I'm so impressed! Did you taste the soup, Beauty? Isn't it amazing?"

She's just staring into her bowl.

I motion for her to eat.

She sighs and takes a small sip off her spoon. "Uh-huh."

I wait for her to say something else, but she doesn't. I guess I'll have to keep talking. "So, Beauty. What do you like to do in your spare time?"

"I read," she says. "A lot."

"Oh, yeah? What about you, Mr. Beast? Do you like to read?"

"Not really," he says.

"What do you like to do?" I ask him.

"I like to cook," he says, and takes a slurp of soup. "And eat. Beasts are hungry all the time. I have multiple meals a day. Breakfast. Brunch. Lunch. Linner. Dinner."

"Linner?" asks Jonah.

"It's between lunch and dinner," Mr. Beast explains.

No wonder his dinner is at nine. He has to build in time for all those extra meals.

"There's also aftinner. After Dinner," Mr. Beast adds.

When does he have time to sleep?

"What else do you like to do?" I ask Mr. Beast.

"Play games," he says. "Like trump."

"And flying crocodile!" Jonah says.

Mr. Beast smiles. "That, too."

"Do you like to play trump?" I ask Beauty.

"I don't know how," she says, taking another spoonful of soup.

"Maybe Mr. Beast can teach you after dinner," I say.

Mr. Beast gives a hint of a nod. "I can. If you want to learn."

"Okay," Beauty says. "I'd like that."

Hurrah! We're in the middle of date number one — dinner! After this, we'll go straight into date number two — playing a game. Maybe we can even top the evening off with date number three — dancing. And they'll be madly in love and we'll be all done.

The main course comes and I'm in food heaven. So is Jonah. Even Beauty is gobbling it down. Mmm. So much cheese. Yum. Maybe it's from Freckles's shop. Good job, Freckles.

I try to keep the conversation going between bites.

"So, Mr. Beast, have you lived in this palace a long time?" I ask.

"No," he says curtly. He takes a big bite of pasta.

I glance at Beauty in case she has any follow-up questions, but she's silent.

These two could really work on their conversational skills. But I'm not ready to give up. "How long have you lived here?" I go on.

"About two years," he says.

"It's very pretty. And quiet."

"I like the quiet," he says. "I like to be far from Town." He takes a gulp of his water and looks up at Beauty. "Do you miss Town?"

It's the first question he's asked her yet.

"I do," she admits. "I used to live there before my dad lost his business and we had to move out to the cottage. I've always dreamt about moving back. It's so vibrant. I like the hustle and bustle. I like to be around lots of people."

"Oh," Beast says. He takes another gulp of water.

Humph. She couldn't have pretended to want to live out here in the middle of nowhere?

Mr. Beast returns to eating.

Watching him eat is kind of strange. His lips are big. His teeth are so sharp. And he can put a lot more pasta in his mouth than any person I've ever seen.

When I see the chocolate cheesecake dessert coming, I motion to Jonah. *Let's go*, I mouth.

He makes a sad face but pushes back his chair.

"Jonah and I don't want dessert," I announce. It's a total lie, but I have to stick to the plan. "You guys go ahead. We're stuffed."

Mr. Beast looks at us suspiciously. "Really? Neither of you

wants to try my delicious chocolate cheesecake? It's extra chocolaty."

A strangled sound escapes Jonah's lips.

"No, thank you," I say, which is difficult, believe me. "You two finish up and then play your game. We'll be upstairs. Have fun!"

Whew. Now they'll really get a chance to talk. They're going to fall in love and live happily ever after. Maybe it'll happen right away and we'll be able to go home before bedtime.

Jonah and I turn and start to walk out of the dining room.

We don't get far before Beauty pushes her chair back. "I need to go upstairs, too. Sorry. I don't think I can play trump tonight. Thank you for dinner."

Huh? What's she doing?

Mr. Beast's face clouds over. "Fine. Good night," he thunders.

Without comment, she runs from the dining room.

Jonah and I just stand there dumbfounded. What just happened?

Mr. Beast looks down at his plate. "I told you she wouldn't like me," he mutters. "She doesn't even want to play cards with me."

"She did! She does!" I exclaim. "I don't know what happened."

"I'll play with you," Jonah says, rushing back to the table. "But can we have the cheesecake first?"

Mr. Beast shrugs.

"I'm going to check on Beauty," I say. I hurry up the grand staircase and knock on Beauty's door.

"Come in," she calls.

"What happened?" I ask as I step inside. She's lying on her bed in a ball, clutching her stomach.

I gasp. "What's wrong?"

"It's the cheese," she says. "I can't eat cheese! I'm allergic!"

Huh? "But you ate the goat cheese soup! And the cheese ravioli! Why did you eat so much cheese? I don't understand."

She sniffs. "I didn't want to insult Mr. Beast by not eating his food. He cooked it."

"But you're sick!"

"I know. When I eat cheese, I get really dizzy and then I feel like I'm going to throw up. I can't go back downstairs. I can barely stand up!"

"Do you need to go to the hospital?" I ask.

"No," she says. "I'll be okay. I just need to go to sleep."

I back slowly out of the room and go downstairs. Jonah and Mr. Beast are in the den, playing cards.

"Is she coming down?" Mr. Beast asks when he sees me. "She ran away so fast, it was as though she was allergic to me."

"It's not you she's allergic to," I say. "It's cheese."

He frowns. "She is? Why didn't she tell me?"

"She didn't want to hurt your feelings." I take the opportunity to further my cause. "That's how much she likes you. She was willing to eat your food even though it made her sick."

"But I don't want someone to suffer because of my food. I don't want someone to suffer at all. Not by eating my food or by being with me."

I don't know what to say to that, so I just stay quiet.

"Maybe I should bring Beauty something to read," I say eventually. "Can she borrow a book?"

"Of course," he says, playing a card. "I have a million books in the basement. I'm not much of a reader, but they were my grandfather's. He always had his nose in a book. I've never even looked through them."

Jonah yawns.

"Jonah, ten more minutes and then you have to go to bed," I say.

"You're not my mother, Abby," he grumbles.

"Maryrose told us that I'm in charge when we're in fairy tale land. You just don't remember."

"She did?"

"Yes," I lie. "It's for your own safety."

"It's almost time for my aftinner anyway," Mr. Beast says. "You should get some sleep, Jonah. Breakfast will be served at seven A.M. sharp."

"What are you making?" I ask.

"A cheeseburger."

"For breakfast?" Gross.

He laughs. "No. For aftinner. Omelets for breakfast."

"Cheese-free, I hope," I say.

"With homemade ketchup?" Jonah asks, licking his lips.

"With homemade ketchup," Mr. Beast promises.

While they finish up their game, I go downstairs to find the books.

The basement is dark and smells musty. I turn on the lamp and see piles and piles of books all over the floor and scattered around messily on the shelves.

I pick up a few books from the top of a pile and bring them upstairs to Beauty.

"There are stacks and stacks of books in the basement," I tell her, handing over the ones I chose. "Mr. Beast says you can read whatever you want. I grabbed you a few. I wasn't sure what kinds you liked."

"I'm too dizzy to read," she says, putting the books on her nightstand. "But thanks. I'll have a look tomorrow."

"You sure you don't want to see a doctor?"

"No, no, tomorrow it will be gone. It always is."

"Always? How often do you eat the thing you're allergic to?"

"A lot," she admits sheepishly. "I don't like to insult anyone."

"Beauty! You can't worry so much about insulting people. You have to worry about yourself!"

She sighs. "Can you lecture me tomorrow? I'm not really up for it."

I pull the covers up to her chin. "Okay, I'll lecture you tomorrow. *Plus* we have a fun day planned. You and Mr. Beast are going to get to know each other really well. I'll bet you'll even fall in love!"

"I'm not sure about *that*," she says. "But I'll stay longer if it helps you. And he has stacks of books. I love books so much. Books are amazing."

"So's Mr. Beast," I press. "He's amazing, too. You'll see."

She closes her eyes without answering.

✳ chapter twelve ✳

Tell Me a Story

I oversleep. The bed is so comfortable. The sheets are silky, and the purple comforter is extra fluffy.

When I open my eyes, the first thing I do is run into the sitting room and check the magic mirror to make sure my parents are still in their bed.

"*Snoooooooooooooooorrrshhhh —*"

This time, the snore belongs to my mom. Their clock says 4:50.

I return to my room, go through the closet, and put on comfy black leggings and a sparkly orange top. Then I go check on Beauty, but she's not in her room. Neither is my brother. I hurry downstairs and find Jonah, Mr. Beast, and Prince at the table, munching away on blueberry pancakes.

I stretch my arms above my head. "Morning. I thought you were making omelets! Where's Beauty?"

"She's in the basement," Jonah says, his mouth full of pancake. "And you missed the omelets. That was breakfast. This is brunch!"

"Jonah, swallow and then speak," I order as I sit down at the table.

He sticks his blueberry-covered tongue out at me.

Mr. Beast laughs.

"What's she doing in the basement?"

"Organizing the books," Mr. Beast says. "She's been at it since six."

"Is she feeling okay?" I wonder.

"Seems so," Mr. Beast says.

"Did you guys play trump yet?" I ask.

"No," Mr. Beast says. "She's been in the basement all morning."

I need to get her to come up. Maybe we should skip playing trump and go directly to dancing. Yeah. That's the most romantic of all the dates. This romance needs a kick in the pants.

I shovel down my pancakes and then go ask Mr. Butler for help setting up.

"Dancing!" he squeals. "Mrs. Butler and I love to dance."

"Great," I cheer. "Where should we do it?" I enunciate very clearly so he understands.

"In the Great Hall?"

"Perfect!" I say. "Can you set up the music? I'll get everyone."

"Splendid!" he cries.

I run down to the basement to find Beauty. "Beauty! Come upstairs! We're going to dance!"

"Now?" she asks. "I'm kind of busy!"

She *is* busy. She's knee-deep in books. "There are so many fantastic reads here," she says. "You have no idea. But they're a mess. I'm organizing them by genre."

"Cool," I say. "Are you almost done?"

She laughs. "Are you kidding? It'll take me a week!"

Hmm. At least she's not running for the hills. "Do you think you can take a quick break for some dancing?"

"I'm not that coordinated," she says.

"I'm sure you're fine," I say. "Come on up! You can organize more afterward."

"Well, all right," she says, dropping a pile of books onto a shelf.

She follows me upstairs. She looks beautiful even though she's all dusty. She's wearing a simple blue dress and matching blue heels.

"Come into the Great Hall," I say.

The Great Hall is a huge room about the size of our house in Smithville. The floor is what I once heard my mom call a harlequin floor — a diamond pattern of white and black.

Mr. Beast, my brother, and Mr. and Mrs. Butler are already waiting for us in the room.

Mr. Beast is grumbling to himself and pretending to stare at the chandelier in the ceiling.

Jonah is playing hopscotch on the tiles.

This is going to work. I know it. Beauty and Mr. Beast will dance, they'll fall in love, and the story will be saved.

"I brought music," Mrs. Butler says. "Let me put on the record player!"

"Let me get the lights," says Mr. Butler.

Mrs. Butler runs off in one direction, Mr. Butler in the other.

Perfect. Some soft music. Romantic lighting . . . that will do the trick!

I hear a scratching sound and then —

Boom, boom, boom!

It's dance music. Loud, bouncy, dance music.

"Wahoo!" Mrs. Butler calls out and starts to wave her arms in the air. "Dance party!"

Wait a sec. I didn't say dance *party*, did I?

A streak of red blazes across the room. And then a streak of green. And yellow. And blue. Mr. Butler has a disco ball. A multi-colored disco ball.

"Party, party, party!" Mr. Butler yells.

"Fun!" Jonah calls out and starts to jump up and down.

"No, no, no," I say. But no one listens.

Now Mr. Beast starts to wiggle his arms overhead, too.

"This is not what I had in mind," I say. "Can we put on something slower?"

Mrs. Butler points to her ear. "I can't hear you! THE MUSIC IS TOO LOUD."

Crumbs.

I march off to the other side of the room to find the record player myself. The record that's playing is in fact labeled FAST DANCE.

I spot a stack of records on the table and flip through them quickly.

MEDIUM DANCE. FAST DANCE 2. SLOW DANCE.

There we go!

I pull FAST DANCE off the record player with a loud scratch.

"Hey!" Mrs. Butler calls. "What happened?"

"Sorry!" I chirp. "It was a little loud. I thought we'd start off with something slightly softer."

I put on SLOW DANCE. A soft melody comes out. It sounds like a lullaby.

Mr. Butler bows and Mrs. Butler curtsies. She goes into his arms and they leisurely waltz across the hall.

Beauty and Mr. Beast stare awkwardly at each other. Neither of them seems to want to make the first move.

I clap my hands like a ballet teacher. "Pair up, pair up. Mr. Beast! Would you mind dancing with Beauty, please?"

Even with all his fur, I can see that he's blushing. "Um, would you like to dance?" he asks her.

She blushes, too. "I guess," she says.

I wish she'd sound a teeny, tiny bit more enthusiastic.

He takes one of her hands in his. He puts his other arm around her waist.

They stare at each other for a beat.

And then — he shuffles to the right. She shuffles to the right.

He shuffles back to the left. She shuffles back to the left. They're dancing! Hurrah!

Now he's looking down at her. He's smiling. She's looking up at him! She's smiling! They're connecting. This is romance!

"Owwwww!" Mr. Beast howls.

They tear apart. Mr. Beast falls to the floor.

"What happened?" I ask, rushing toward him.

"I'm so sorry," Beauty cries. "I stepped on his foot with my heel! He's not wearing shoes. Why aren't you wearing shoes?"

"We're in my house," Mr. Beast barks. "Why would I wear shoes in my own house?"

"Because we're dancing!" she says, biting her thumbnail.

"Easy for you to say; you have human feet," he retorts. "Shoes don't fit my beast feet properly. But I'm *fine.* Thanks for asking."

"I'm really sorry," she says, hanging her head. "I told Abby I wasn't very coordinated."

"I'm not, either," he grumbles. "Why are we dancing, anyway?"

I've had enough. ENOUGH. I clench my fists and yell, "Because I am trying to make you guys fall in love! I am trying to make you fall in love so you'll get married! But you're making it very difficult for me! VERY, VERY DIFFICULT!"

"Get married?" Beauty repeats, her eyes wide. She takes a giant step back.

"Yes," I say. I draw in a deep breath. I think I spooked her.

"It's not going to happen," Mr. Beast snaps. "I told you, Abby. Forget about it. You should just go home. All of you. Abby. Beauty. Jonah."

"Me?" Jonah asks. "You want me to leave, too?"

"You too," he says. "I should never have kept you against your will. You have a real home. You should return to it."

"We're not going anywhere yet," I say.

"Yes, you are," Mr. Beast insists. "Okay, look. I'm hungry and it's lunchtime and no matter what, I'm a good host, so I will prepare lunch. A cheeseless lunch." He sighs at the thought. "But then after that, I want you all to vacate the premises." He hops on his good foot out of the Great Hall.

Mr. and Mrs. Butler follow him out.

Beauty looks at me with a question in her eyes. "Married? You never said anything about our getting married."

"You're right," I admit. "But that was always my plan. I wanted him to fall in love with you and ask you to marry him."

She bites her thumbnail again. "But I'm not in love with him."

"Not *yet*," I say. "But you will be! You two are a perfect match!"

"How?" she asks. "We don't have anything in common. Don't people who get married usually have things in common?"

"Opposites attract," Jonah exclaims. "Isn't that an expression Nana sometimes says, Abby?"

"Yes!" I say. "It is. Opposites attract."

Beauty continues biting her nail. She looks skeptical.

I have to make her come around! But how? What does she like?

The answer comes to me. She likes helping.

"Marrying Mr. Beast would be a really good deed," I say. And it's not even a lie. "A REALLY good deed. And you like to do good deeds, right?"

She nods.

"I need him to ask you to marry him. And I need you to say yes. It's a good deed. A selfless deed! It would be a mitzvah!"

"A what?"

"A really good deed!" Jonah says.

"But I wasn't planning on staying here forever," Beauty says. "I have to get to Soup Kitchen. And Grumpy Great-Grandma. And the orphans need me. And my dad will be home soon. Who's going to help him run the cottage?"

"Don't you have two sisters?" I ask. "They can help!"

"They never help," she says. "I have to do everything."

"Let them do it! And other people can work at the soup kitchen. And help orphans. And Grumpy Great-Grandma. Doesn't she have great-grandkids? Where are they?"

"They're not that nice," Beauty says. "They're Grumpy Great-Grandkids."

"Well, it's time everyone else pulled their weight. We need you here. We appreciate you here. Please say yes. Please say you'll marry Mr. Beast if he asks. I can't tell you why, but it is so, so important. And he really, really wants to marry you."

She hesitates. "Well . . ."

"Pretty pretty pretty please?" Jonah asks.

"Okay," she says with a sigh.

I throw my arms around her. "Yay! Thank you!"

One down. One to go.

chapter thirteen

The Curse

"anyone want to play flying crocodile before we go?" Jonah asks as we exit the Great Hall.

"We're not going anywhere yet," I say. "First we have to fix this. I'm going to help Mr. Beast cook."

"And I'm going back downstairs to organize the books." Beauty turns to Jonah. "Want to help?"

"I don't really like books," my brother says.

"Then you haven't found the *right* books. I bet I can change your mind," Beauty says in a singsong voice.

"I bet you can't," Jonah sings back.

"I'll tell you what," Beauty says, her hands on her hips. "Let me pick out one book for you. You have to read it. If you don't like it, then you were right. If you do like it, then I was right."

"What do I get if I'm right?" Jonah asks.

Beauty shrugs. "You don't have to read anything for the rest of your life."

What? Huh?

"Deal!" Jonah squeals.

I wave my hand. "Um, hang on. I'm not sure if my parents would agree to that plan."

"Too late!" Jonah cries. "I already said 'deal.' What happens if I lose?"

Beauty smiles. "It's a surprise."

Jonah narrows his eyes. "I normally like surprises, but I'm suspicious of this one."

"Don't be. Promise." She winks at me and runs down the stairs. "And you already said 'deal.'"

I let them go, a little worried. I find Mr. Beast in the kitchen, cutting a chicken breast into strips.

It's one of the biggest kitchens I've ever seen. It has two sinks, two ovens, and two oversized fridges. There are spices everywhere.

Basil, oregano, cinnamon. Or is it spelled *cinamon*? *Cinnamon*? Uch, never mind.

I look into the empty pan. "What are you making?"

"Chicken stir-fry," he says brusquely.

"Can I help?" I ask. I use my extra-sweet voice.

I wait for him to tell me to go away, but instead he shrugs. "If you want to. The aprons are on the back of the door."

Hurrah! I'm in. I wash my hands in the sink, pull a long brown apron off the hook, and tie it behind me. It goes past my feet.

"Have you always liked to cook?" I ask, stepping closer and trying not to trip.

He makes some space for me on the counter and hands me a cutting board, a knife, and a carrot. "Chop," he says. Then he adds, "My dad and I used to cook together."

"Is he . . . dead?" I ask while chopping very, very carefully. One birthday gift I know my mother absolutely wouldn't want is half my finger. Missing a finger wouldn't help with my painting skills, either.

"No," Mr. Beast eventually answers. "My parents and older brothers live in another kingdom."

"Oh," I say, surprised. "Is Another Kingdom the name of their kingdom?"

"Huh? No." He laughs. "It's called the kingdom of Horatio. Only *this* kingdom has weird names. I wasn't born with the name Beast, either."

"What's your real name?" I ask.

"Mike."

I snort-laugh. "Mike? That's so normal-sounding!"

"Yeah, well, I was normal back then," he says wistfully. He pours some oil into the pan. For the first time, I notice that he has only three fingers on each hand. Well, really more like a claw than a hand. I bet that doesn't help *his* painting skills.

"Why did you move away?" I ask. "Was your family scared of you?" As soon as the words leave my mouth, I want to suck them back in. How rude! "Not that you're scary. You're not scary. Nope. You're the opposite of scary. You're calming. Like a scented candle. Or diaper rash cream." I don't know where that last one came from. Although I do have vivid memories of my parents having to buy a lot of diaper rash cream for my brother.

"It's okay. I *know* I look scary," Mr. Beast says. "But that's not why I left. My family was never afraid of me. They pitied me. And they kept trying to set me up with different girls. My mom

even gave me her emerald engagement ring to propose to someone with. But I never got the chance. The girls would take one
look at me and freak out. One literally ran out of our palace cry-
ing when she first saw me."

"That must have hurt your feelings," I say, feeling terrible for
Mr. Beast.

He nods. "And it really upset my parents," he says. "So when
I was eighteen, I moved out here to my grandad's empty castle. I
changed my name. That's that."

"That is so sad," I say. "Although it is a nice castle."

"Yes," he says. "It suits me to be in the middle of nowhere.
I'm a homebody. And I love the big kitchen. I like cooking. I like
cooking for lots of people."

"Good. Because my brother and I like to eat. And we don't
want to go yet, either. Can we all stay a little longer? Please?"

"To be honest, I do like having you all as guests. It's nice to
have someone besides Mr. and Mrs. Butler to talk to. Not sure if
you noticed, but they don't hear that well." He plunks the chicken
into the pan.

"I've noticed," I say.

The chicken sizzles.

I clear my throat. "Mr. Beast, why did you get cursed?"

He tenses. "Excuse me?"

"Why did the fairy curse you? What did you do?"

He sighs. "I didn't do anything. Nothing. Jax — the fairy — just cursed me."

Jax. I remember Mr. Beast stomping his foot and mentioning Jax when Jonah and I arrived at the castle.

"You must have done *something*," I say. "Were you mean to him?"

"Not that I know of. I hope not. I was just a regular prince. I had seen Jax around my kingdom once or twice, but I didn't know him well. And then one day, I went into the garden and there he was. Sitting in a tree. I'll tell you what he said when he cursed me." Mr. Beast puts down his spatula and leans closer to me. "He said that I was too handsome and too rich and I had it too easy and that it just wasn't fair. And the next thing I knew, *poof*, I was a beast."

I feel a sinking feeling in my stomach. "So he did it because he was jealous?"

He nods. "I guess so. Jealousy makes people do horrible things."

My face burns. "It does. It really does. What happened next?" I ask.

"Jax explained the curse. He said I would only go back to my regular self if and only if I convinced someone to marry me. The catch is that they couldn't know that I'd been cursed. Which makes breaking the curse pretty much impossible. Because who would want to marry an ugly animal?" He frowns and covers the pot with a lid.

I stand up straight. "Mr. Beast, that's what I want to talk to you about. Beauty *will* marry you. I asked her and she said she would! She likes you!" I say. Okay, fine, she doesn't *exactly* like him, but she doesn't *not* like him.

And now that I know the curse was because of jealousy, I feel even more pressure to make it right.

Mr. Beast shakes his head. "She doesn't like me. She stomped on my foot!"

"The foot-stomping was an accident," I say. "Promise me you'll give her a chance. All you have to do is ask her to marry you and you get your happy ending! Don't you want your happy ending?"

He hesitates.

"Hi, guys." Beauty appears at the door to the kitchen. "I picked out a book for you, Abby. I have it in the other room."

"Oh, thanks," I say.

"I picked out one for you, too, Mr. Beast," Beauty says.

Mr. Beast looks up in surprise. "You did?"

"I know you said you're not much of a reader, but in this book, the main character is a chef and there are recipes sprinkled throughout the book. And some magic." She blushes. "You don't have to read it if you don't want to. But I was looking for books for Jonah, and I thought you might enjoy this one."

Mr. Beast also blushes. "Thank you," he says.

"Isn't she thoughtful?" I say. "And sweet! So sweet!"

"Very thoughtful," he says.

"Did you give a book to Jonah?" I ask.

Beauty nods proudly. "I did. It's called *Blue*. It's about a boy and a crocodile."

"That sounds perfect for him," I say. "Is he reading it?"

"He said it looked boring but a deal's a deal and he promised to try it." She grins. "He's been reading for at least forty minutes now."

"He has?" I'm shocked. Jonah never sits still and reads. Wow.

"Do you need help?" Beauty asks us.

"No, we're good," Mr. Beast says. "It will be ready in a few minutes. We'll come get you. Thank you again for the book."

She smiles. "You're welcome."

"See?" I say after Beauty leaves. "I told you she likes you!"

He shrugs, but I can see he's also smiling.

When our stir-fry is ready, we bring the food out to the table.

I pop my head into the living room, where Jonah and Beauty are both reading books on the sofa. "Jonah, Beauty, lunch is ready."

Neither of them looks up.

"Hey, Jonah?"

No response.

"Jonah?"

He turns a page. "Hmm?"

"Lunch!"

He nods.

"Are you coming?"

He nods.

"We made chicken stir-fry."

He nods again.

"It's chicken and ketchup stir-fry," I say to get his attention.

"Uh-huh."

"With ketchup ice cream."

"Uh-huh."

"Dipped in ketchup."

No response.

"Jonah!" I call out. "I guess you like the book?"

He looks up for a second and then looks back down. "I do! I really do! But I only have two chapters left! Can I read at the table?"

"Sure," I say, surprised.

He brings his book to the table and almost trips as he walks.

Beauty sets down her book and joins us.

Jonah sits in his seat and continues to read.

"This is delicious," Beauty says, taking a bite of chicken stir-fry. "Mr. Beast, you're really a terrific chef."

Mr. Beast smiles. "Thank you. I had help." He nods at me.

Jonah closes the book with a happy sigh. "That was amazing!"

"You're done?" I ask, shocked.

"Yes!"

"But I've never seen you read a book that fast!"

"I know!" Jonah exclaims, digging into his stir-fry.

"What was it about?" I ask him.

"A blue crocodile! And I know crocodiles aren't really blue, but it's fiction! It's an adventure about a little boy named Levi whose best friend is a blue crocodile! And they meet pirates! And mermaids! And they go through magic underwater tunnels!" Jonah's eyes are sparkling.

"No way!" I say.

"Way." He frowns. "But now I'm sad."

"Why? You should be happy! You found a book you like!"

His face squishes. "But it's finished."

Aw. "You can read it again," I say.

He gives me a funny look. "Why would I do that? I already know what happens."

"But it's still fun. I've read each of the fairy tales lots of times. I learn something new every time. Speaking of which, maybe you could read those next. Maybe that will spark some memories."

"Maybe," he says, but he's flipping through his *Blue* book.

"You can read it again, or you can read fairy tales," Beauty says, and then pauses. "Or you can read the sequel."

Jonah's eyes pop out of his head. "There's another one?"

"There are ten. It's a series." Beauty smiles. "That's your surprise for losing the bet and liking the book!"

"No way!" Jonah cheers. "That's the best news I've ever heard!"

We all laugh.

Mr. Beast looks around the table. "This is . . . fun."

"See?" I say. "I told you! Does that mean we can stay a little longer?"

He nods. "You can. In fact . . ." He glances across the table at Beauty. "I'm wondering if *you'll* stay for good."

"For good?" she repeats. Her fork clatters against her plate.

Mr. Beast stands up. He crosses the space between them in three giant steps. He gets down on one knee.

My heart thumps in anticipation. He's on one knee! Does this mean what I think it means? Yes, yes, yes!

Mr. Beast clears his throat. He holds an emerald engagement ring in his furry fingers. "Beauty, will you marry me?"

* chapter fourteen *

The Change

he asked! He did it! He proposed on one knee! His face is looking so hopeful, too! Yay! I bop in my seat. As soon as Beauty accepts, the curse is undone.

Right?

Yes.

Unless I somehow messed it up. By, um, urging her to accept.

I swallow hard. I hope I didn't mess it up.

Beauty's eyes are wide. She opens her mouth to say something but then closes it.

Is she going to say no? After all this, she BETTER not say no!

"I . . . I . . . I . . ." Her eyes tear up. "Yes. I will marry you."

She said yes! Hurrah!

He proposed! She said yes!

Mr. Beast slips the engagement ring onto her finger.

How romantic!

Well, not *exactly* romantic. They're not *exactly* in love. I kind of forced them into it. But it's for their own good. Hopefully. And they *will* be in love. Eventually. Won't they? *This better work, this better work, this better work.*

Just as I begin to doubt myself, Mr. Beast starts to sparkle.

Yes. Sparkle.

His brown fur shimmers and disappears. He starts to shrink, too. He gets smaller and smaller until he's a normal height.

A normal height and suddenly very, very handsome.

Wow. Mr. Beast is gorgeous!

He has black hair, smooth olive skin, and a chiseled chin. He looks like a movie star.

Beauty's jaw drops. "Who are you?"

Mr. Beast touches his bare cheeks. "It's me!"

"Who's me?" she asks. "What happened to Mr. Beast?" She glances at me. "Why is this guy so handsome?"

"It worked?" Mr. Beast asks, incredulous. "I'm handsome?"

"It worked!" I holler, jumping out of my chair. "You're really, really handsome!"

I did it! I'm a genius!

Jonah jumps up, too, and we high-five.

"What's going on?" Beauty asks. "Can someone tell me what's happening? I'm kind of freaked out! Who is this guy? What happened to Mr. Beast?"

"*I'm* Mr. Beast!" he says. "Or maybe not technically anymore. I guess I can go back to being Mike."

"You should be Mr. Handsome," Beauty says.

Mr. Beast/Mike/Mr. Handsome runs to a mirror behind the dining room table. "I never thought I'd see my skin again!" he exclaims.

"Can someone please explain what's going on?" Beauty asks. "I'm very confused!"

I turn to Beauty. "A fairy named Jax cursed Mr. Beast — I mean Mike — and told him that he would be a beast unless he proposed and had his proposal accepted! And he did! And you did! And now he's back to normal! He's a handsome prince!"

"Why didn't anyone tell me that?" she asks.

"We couldn't. That was part of the curse. You weren't

allowed to know. You had to agree to marry him even though he looked like a beast."

She bites her lower lip and turns to Mike. "But does that mean you only asked me to marry you because you wanted to get rid of the curse?"

He looks reluctantly away from the reflection. "Well . . . mostly. But you do seem really nice. You even picked out a book you thought I'd like. And Abby thinks we were meant to be together. She said you liked me and wanted me to ask. You're the only girl who has ever liked me even though I looked like a beast."

I can't help but squirm. That's not exactly what happened. Their entire relationship is based on lies and arm-twisting.

Maybe they shouldn't be getting married?

I glance at Mike. No. He's back to being handsome! And she's Beauty. These two are meant to be together. It might just take a little time for the real love to bloom.

"When's the wedding?" Jonah asks.

Now Beauty and Mike are the ones with frog eyes.

"Um . . ." they both mutter.

"Can you do it tonight?" Jonah asks. "Because I bet it will be fun and we really do have to go home soon. Right, Abby?"

"Yes," I say. "We do. Tonight would be really convenient for us. If you can swing it."

I guess we could leave before the wedding. Mr. Beast — Mike — is already back to normal even if they don't get married. Although maybe the curse comes back if they don't?

Better to make sure all loose ends are tied before we leave. I'd hate to go home and see a miserable Beauty and a depressed Beast on my jewelry box.

"I guess we can do it tonight," Mike says with a big smile. "I'll make us a wedding feast for dinner! And we'll invite the whole kingdom."

"My father is traveling," Beauty says, and hangs her head. "And my sisters won't come."

"Their loss," Mike says.

"I'm sure everyone else in Kingdom will come when they hear you're getting married, Beauty," I say. "Everyone loves you!"

Mike nods. "Beauty, I am forever in your debt, for agreeing to marry me and changing me back."

She beams for the first time. "My pleasure. Happy to help."

"Shall I send Mr. Butler back to your house to collect all your things?" Mike offers. "Since you'll be staying for good?"

She blinks. "Here?" she repeats. She blinks again.

"Yes," he says, looking at her strangely. "Here. Your new home."

"Oh. Right." She gnaws on her thumb. "My new home. Yes. Please. You can send Mr. Butler to fetch my stuff."

"Perfect," I say, ignoring Beauty's obvious concern. "Jonah and I will stay for the wedding and then go home through the mirror. Everything is set."

I get to dress up for a wedding! Yay! I'll wear the fancy purple satin dress in my closet. It'll be perfect. Maybe I can even wear it home?

"Should we do it in the Great Hall?" Mike asks.

"Ruff! Ruff, ruff!"

"Where's Prince?" Jonah asks.

"It sounds like he's outside," I say. "Maybe he's trying to tell us the wedding should be in the garden. I'll go see what he's up to. Prince?" I call, heading outside. "Everything okay?"

"Ruff, ruff, ruff!"

Wow, it got cold out here. And it looks like it's about to rain. I guess we should have the wedding inside.

"Prince?" I shout. "Where are you? Come inside, it's going to pour!"

"Ruff!"

I spot Prince standing under a tree, pawing at the air and barking. Loudly.

"Prince, what are you barking at? Is it a bird?"

He barks even louder.

"Prince! Stop it!"

"I'm not a bird," says a booming voice.

Huh?

I look up to see a young man swinging from one of the branches. He is wearing a striped blue-and-white suit. He has purple hair.

"Howdy!" he says.

"Hello," I say. I feel that creepy-crawly feeling down my back. "Do I know you?"

He's holding a silver-and-red yo-yo in his hand and he throws it up and down and up and down. "I'm Jax."

Jax? Who's Jax? Wait! "You're the jealous fairy who cursed Mr. Beast!"

✶ chapter fifteen ✶

Jax Strikes Back

I take a quick step back.

"Jealous?" Jax pouts. "You're right. I was jealous. He had everything. Wealth. Health. Extreme good looks. And he was even nice. All the girls wanted to marry him. They used to line up on the streets to meet him! Did anyone line up on the streets to meet me? No. Never! And I have magical powers! Did anyone care? No one cared! They all liked him for his looks! Blah. I had to do something about it."

I hug myself and glare at Jax. "You *did* do something about it. You cursed him."

He cackles. "Yes. And he was *only* supposed to turn back when a woman agreed to marry him despite his beastly looks."

"She did!" I call out. "Beauty agreed to marry him! And she didn't know about the curse! I swear!"

"I know, I know," Jax sighs. "That's why he changed back. I couldn't stop it." He flips over and hangs from the branch by his knees. "But! But, but, but. She didn't agree to marry him because she loved him for who he was, now, did she?"

I clear my throat. "Well, not exactly . . ."

"Tsk, tsk, tsk," he says. He wags his finger at me. "She doesn't love him! She agreed to marry him because you told her it was a good *deed*. And Beauty is quite the do-gooder, isn't she? Orphans, soup kitchens, grumpy great-grandmas. You took advantage of her, didn't you? You preyed on her weakness and found a loophole in my curse."

My shoulders tense. "I guess. Maybe. But I had to. And what difference does it make? They were going to fall in love anyway."

"Maybe. Maybe not. But I'll tell you what. Your shenanigans annoy me. A lot. I think you deserve to be punished. Do you think you deserve to be punished?"

A wave of dread washes over me.

"No!" I cry. "Don't punish me!" But even as I say the words, a deep-down part of me *does* think I deserve to be punished.

Not for tricking Beauty into agreeing to marry Mr. Beast.

But for ruining Penny's painting.

Jax lets his yo-yo swing from side to side. "Too bad," he says gleefully. "You're getting punished!" He clears his throat and chants, *"With magic from north, south, west, and east, I shall turn you into a beast!"*

I gasp. A beast? Wait! Wait wait wait! "No!" I shout. "Don't turn me into a beast!"

But it's too late. I feel tingles all over my body. From my toes to my head to my fingers. And then I feel like I'm stretching. And growing.

Growing hair.

Growing hair?

I'm growing hair! On my hands! I don't want to grow hair on my hands!

My hands are covered in hair. My arms are covered in hair. My legs are covered in hair. I am still wearing my clothes, but every part of my skin is covered in fur! I am furry!

I hear a loud howling.

Is that me?

With relief, I realize that it isn't. It's Prince. He's looking at me and howling. Which is also pretty alarming.

Jax is laughing hysterically. "You took away my last beast, so now *you're* a beast!"

"But I don't want to be a beast!" I say, and I realize it's hard to talk around my fangs.

FANGS! Agh!

Jax laughs again. "Tough luck!"

I'm panicking and my heart is racing under my furry chest. "But I have to go back to Smithville tonight! I can't go back to Smithville as a beast!"

"Too bad!" Jax cackles.

"But there are no beasts in Smithville!"

He hangs upside down so his purple hair flops over. "There will be now!"

I want to cry. I thought I had figured everything out, but now everything is a mess! I am covered in fur. I have to turn back into me.

"Wait!" I shout at Jax. "There has to be a way out. There's always an out. Right? Mr. Beast had to get someone to marry him. What do I have to do? And it can't be getting someone to marry me, because I'm only ten!"

Jax snorts. "You want an out? Okay, how's this? Stop Beauty from marrying Mr. Beast. They don't really love each other, anyway. If they break their engagement, he'll turn back into a beast. Forever. But you'll be free. Good luck! Hah!" He pulls himself up by the branch and disappears right into the tree.

Prince looks up at me. I look down at him.

He barks. Then he whimpers. Then he starts to howl again.

This time I start to howl, too.

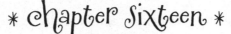

✴ chapter Sixteen ✴

Do Not Look in the Mirror

I run straight back into the house and toward the mirror in the dining room.

I hear gasps all around me as I run.

"An animal broke into the palace!" Beauty cries. "Get it, get it!"

"A-Abby?" Jonah stammers. "Is that you?"

"Oh, no!" screams Mike.

When I see my reflection, it's my turn to gasp.

Is that really me?

I raise my hand. A beast raises its hand.

I raise my other hand. A beast raises its other hand.

I stare intently at my reflection. I look like a dog. An upright dog. My nose is black and wrinkly. I have fur all over my face. I have whiskers.

I'm also really tall! My black leggings end at my knees. And my long and hairy arms look ridiculous sticking out of my orange sleeves! Oh no oh no oh no!

"Did Jax do that?" Mike cries.

I nod, speechless.

Mike runs outside, toward the garden. "I will get him," he growls, except it doesn't sound so scary now that he's no longer a beast.

"I'm coming with you!" Beauty cries and follows him out the door.

"What happened?" Jonah asks. I see him behind me in the mirror. His eyes are huge and froglike again.

"Jax cursed me for messing with his spell," I sob, wetting the fur on my cheeks with tears.

"It's, um, not that b-b-bad," my brother stammers.

"It is so!" I say. I try to breathe but am almost hyperventilating. "I can't stay like this!"

"Is there any way to switch back?" Jonah asks.

"If I get Mike and Beauty to break their engagement," I say through my tears. "Which I can't do. You saw how miserable he was as a beast. He's supposed to marry Beauty and stay handsome."

Jonah squeezes my hand. "But, Abby, didn't you say we sometimes change the stories?"

I take a deep breath. "Yes, but that doesn't mean ruining their lives. And if he goes back to being a beast, his life will be ruined."

My shoulders slump.

Maybe being a beast isn't that bad, I tell myself. I glance back at my furry reflection in the mirror. Nope. It's that bad.

I am a gigantic walking dog! With fangs! What am I going to do? I can't go home like this!

Happy birthday, Mom! Surprise! I got you a pet. Me!

I feel sick. What if I'm stuck like this forever?

Maybe my mom can fix it. She'll take me to her hair salon. Maybe a manicurist can fix my claws? And there must be something we can do about all the hair on my face. Waxing?

"He's gone," Mike says, coming back inside. "He's a slippery little fellow. I haven't seen him since he cursed me all those years ago. He just runs around different kingdoms causing havoc in people's lives."

"Poor Abby," Beauty says, hugging me. "What can we do?"

"I don't know," I say.

"Should we postpone the wedding?" Beauty asks. "While we figure this out?"

"No," I say quickly. "We have to stick to the plan. You guys need to get married. And Jonah and I need to get home."

"We'll think of something, Abby," Jonah says. "We will."

I am not feeling very hopeful. I stare at my reflection in the mirror.

A beast stares back.

✲ chapter seventeen ✲

Three Fingers Are Not Enough Fingers

by four o'clock I still have no plan.

And I am still a beast.

My fur is making me really itchy.

My shoes don't fit.

My bottom lip is sore because I keep biting it with my fangs.

My clothes are too tight and too short.

Also, I am starving.

"Time for linner," Mike tells me. "You're going to want a lot of meals. Beasts need a lot of fuel. Let me make you some spaghetti."

Jonah and I are sitting on stools in the kitchen. Beauty is downstairs in the basement, still sorting the books.

"Okay," I say with a pout.

There are all kinds of things baking in the ovens and boiling on the stoves right now. Mike is cooking up a storm for the wedding, which will be in just a few hours.

He hands me a plate of spaghetti and a fork.

"Thanks," I say. But when I try to use my fork to twirl my spaghetti, I can't figure out how to use it. I have only three fingers. Why? I don't know. I am missing my pinkie and ring fingers. Where did they go? I would like them back! How does one do anything with three fingers?

I drop the fork onto my plate with a frustrated bang.

"Forget the fork," Mike says sheepishly. "It took me a year to learn to use a fork. Just eat with your hands. I don't mind."

"But —"

"I want to try, too!" Jonah squeals. "I love eating with my hands. Can I please have some spaghetti, Mr. Beast? I mean, Mike."

"Sure!" Mike makes Jonah a plate, too. And one for himself.

The three of us lean over our plates, and we all eat with our hands.

Much easier.

Normally, I'd yell at Jonah for having bad table manners, but there's really not much I can say now, is there?

"There's something missing," Mike says, sniffing the food. "But I can't tell. My nose isn't the same."

"It's still delicious," I say, slurping noodles. Mmm.

"Thanks," Mike says. He takes another bite of meatball. "I'm still full from lunch, though. What a waste. As a regular man, I can't really eat linner anymore."

"Hey, Abby?" Jonah says, happily munching away. "Do you want to change your name to something with 'beast' in it? Something girlier than 'Beast.' Like 'Beastette.'"

I spit out a chunk of meatball. "I do not want my name to be Beastette," I snap.

"Beastella?"

"No."

"Being a beast really isn't that bad," Mike says.

"It seems pretty bad," I say.

"Well, you never get cold," he points out. "Winter is coming. It's getting chilly outside. You'll be warm just as you are, but I'll need a sweater."

"I'd rather wear a sweater," I say, scratching my arms. So itchy!

"I miss my sense of smell," Mike says. "I feel blind without it. Handsome, but blind." He stands up and sniffs one of his pots. "Cooking isn't the same."

"I guess. But I don't really cook." I try to slurp up a noodle but end up stabbing my bottom lip with my fang. I need to switch back. But how? "I wonder if there's another fairy who can help me. Are you inviting any fairies to the wedding?"

"The only fairy I know is Jax," Mike huffs. "And he's *not* invited. He's dangerous."

"Good point," I say. "I guess I could ask Maryrose. She's a fairy who lives in our mirror. She's kind of helpful. Sometimes. Maybe she'll turn me back."

Not that she helped Jonah regain his memory.

Maryrose does what she wants, when she wants it. We don't know why she does what she does, either. Besides the fact that she brings us into fairy tales, she's a complete mystery to us.

Maybe she won't help me at all.

I'll have to go to school as a beast.

Everyone will laugh at me.

Even Robin and Frankie.

And definitely Penny.

You can stop the wedding, a little voice inside me says.

No. No, no, no! There has to be another way.

There isn't! the little voice inside shrieks. *Stop the wedding! If you stop the wedding, then Mr. Beast will become a beast again and you will go back to normal!*

I block the voice out.

Stopping the wedding of two people who are supposed to be together just to save myself would *really* make me a monster. And I am not a monster! Despite what I look like. Despite the fact that I ruined Penny's painting.

I'm not, I'm not!

I finish my linner and march into the Great Hall to make sure the wedding setup is going well.

Mr. and Mrs. Butler are lighting candles and hanging white streamers. Good.

I head upstairs. In my closet, I find the pretty purple satin dress. I take a deep breath. I put it on.

It's a little short. And with all that extra fur, it doesn't zip up all the way in back. But it's on.

I go to the mirror in the sitting room.

Sigh.

I look ridiculous. Absolutely ridiculous. The dress is way too tight and my fur is bursting out of the seams.

But what can I do? I'm Beastella.

My parents are still in the mirror, too, but now they're in the corner. At least they're still sleeping. Their clock says six o'clock. It's getting late.

What do I do?

You could stop the wedding.

No.

Yes.

No.

I have to just go through with it. If I have to be Beastella for the rest of my life, then that's my punishment.

I deserve it.

✳ chapter eighteen ✳

Time Is Tickin'

In my full Beastella glory, I head to Beauty's room to check on her. She's not there. Is she still downstairs?

I hurry to the basement. "Beauty?" I say. "What are you doing?"

She's dusty and wearing sweatpants and sitting among big piles of books. "There is such great stuff here!"

"Yeah," I say. "But are you going to get ready? You're getting married in an hour."

"I just have a few more books to look through," she says.

She doesn't seem excited. Shouldn't she be at least a little excited to get married?

I don't think she really likes Mike. At all.

I can tell her not to get married. I can tell her that Mike isn't the right guy for her.

Which might be true.

Is it true?

"Beauty?"

"Yeah?"

No. I can't. "You have to get ready. People are going to be here soon."

I leave before I change my mind.

There's a knock at the front door as I climb upstairs.

"I'll get it," I call out.

A group of people dressed in fancy clothes for the wedding stand outside.

"Hello," I say. "Please go to the Great Hall."

There's silence. And then, "AHHHHHH!" They all scream. Then they turn around and run away.

Huh? What just happened?

Oh. I happened. They're screaming because of me. I am a beast in a purple satin dress. I am terrifying.

"Come back!" I call. But they don't. They keep running.

Mrs. Butler puts her hand on my shoulder. "Er, dear, maybe you shouldn't be the official wedding greeter. Why don't you go check on Beauty?"

"I guess so," I say with a sigh.

"Snow?" she asks. "No dear, not yet. But it is quite chilly out."

I hurry to the basement and find Beauty still in sweatpants, still reading.

"Beauty! The wedding is going to start any minute! You have to get ready!"

"Oh my gosh," she says, jumping up. "I lost track of time. There are just so many great books. Should I bring some up for the wedding guests? Would they want to read them?"

"They want to see you get *married*," I tell her. "That's why they're here."

"Of course, of course," Beauty says. "I guess I have to put on my dress. Give me two minutes!"

Beauty runs up the stairs and I follow.

In the entrance hall, I hide behind a tall oval vase as the guests continue to arrive. I don't want to scare anyone else.

"This better be quick," one of the guests grumbles as she slams her way through the foyer, banging the marble with her cane.

Oh! It's Grumpy Great-Grandma!

At the same time, Beauty makes her way down the grand stair-case. I gasp. She looks totally gorgeous. Not that I'm surprised. She's wearing a long, flowy, silky white dress and a white veil. Her hair is loose around her shoulders.

"Ready!" she chimes, stepping onto the floor.

"There you are," snaps Grumpy Great-Grandma. She points her cane at Beauty. "Where have you been? I need more bananas! Right now!"

"Oh, hi," Beauty says. She bites her thumbnail. "Right now?"

Grumpy Great-Grandma bangs her cane against the marble floor. "Yes! Right now!"

Beauty pivots. "Okay, let me just look in the kitchen . . ."

"Beauty, no!" I say, jumping out from my hiding place. "You need to get to the Great Hall. You're getting married. We can find Grumpy Great-Grandma a banana afterward!"

Grumpy Great-Grandma stares at me. Her eyes widen. She screams. She drops her cane, spins on her sneakers, and runs right back out the castle door.

"Guess her hip isn't that bad," I say.

"Careful, Grumpy Great-Grandma, careful!" Beauty calls. "Should I go after her?"

The music starts in the Great Hall. I recognize it from this morning. It's "Slow Dance." I also see bursts of color through the door. Apparently, Mr. and Mrs. Butler are using the disco ball.

"No, Beauty!" I say, closing the castle door. "You're getting married. Now. Let's go."

"Where's Mr. Beast — I mean, Mike?" she asks, looking around.

"I'm here," he says. He's standing by the kitchen door. He's wearing a black suit with a gray sweater over it. He's also wearing a gray scarf. He seems to be really missing his fur.

Jonah is next to him in a suit, the messed-up suspenders, and a purple bow tie that I think is on sideways. He looks adorable. Even Prince is wearing a bow tie.

"Hi," Beauty says shyly.

"Hi," Mike says. But he's not smiling. He's looking at his hands.

"Ready to get married?" Beauty asks.

"I, um, guess so," he says. Now he's wringing his hands.

Last chance, I tell myself. *They're not really in love. I can stop the wedding. I can undo my curse.*

No.

I stand up tall. I will not break up their wedding for myself. I don't want to be that kind of person.

"Let's go," I order. "Both of you. To the Great Hall. To your wedding!"

"All right," Mike says.

"After you," says Beauty.

Neither of them moves.

"Wait," Jonah calls out.

We all turn to him.

He flicks his lopsided suspenders with his thumbs. "You can't get married! If you break the engagement, Abby can turn back into a regular person."

"Jonah, no!" I say. "I told you not to tell them!"

"Sorry, Abby. But they can't get married. And that's that." He swipes his hands together.

"You don't know what you're doing, Jonah!" I cry. "You don't know how fairy tales work. Mom and Dad will be waking up soon! We have to leave! And Mike and Beauty need to have a happy ending!"

"I know they do," Jonah says. "But this isn't it. They shouldn't be getting married. Our plan didn't work."

"What are you talking about?" I say. "Of course it did! They're engaged!"

Jonah shakes his head. "But they're not *in love*."

Mike hangs his head. "He's right. The little man is right. Beauty . . ." His voice chokes up. "We shouldn't go through with this."

"We shouldn't?" she asks.

"No," he says. "I'm not in love with you. And I don't think you're in love with me. I think you felt sorry for me. Am I wrong?"

She hesitates.

Mike takes both her hands in his. "Agreeing to marry me was very kind of you. And I will always be grateful. But we don't have much in common. I like cards. You like books. I like cheese. Cheese makes you sick and dizzy. I want to live in the middle of nowhere. You want to live in Town. We're not a good match."

"But sometimes opposites attract," I squeak.

"Not always," Jonah says.

Beauty exhales. "So we're not getting married." She looks completely . . . relieved.

I'll admit it. I feel completely relieved, too. "But wait. Mike, if you break off the engagement, you're going to turn back into a beast!" I tell him.

He nods. "I assumed so."

"But this time, it will be forever. You won't be able to switch back. There won't be a way out."

He nods again. "Abby, I spent *years* comparing myself to normal people. Years. And what I didn't realize until now was that it's not so bad being a beast. I always stayed warm. I had a great sense of smell. I could cook more because I ate more. You want to know the truth? I miss my fangs."

"But —"

"No *but*s. It's what I want. And I want to help you."

My cheeks burn. "But you can't break your engagement because of *me*. I don't deserve it."

"It's not *just* because of you. I really do miss being a beast. But, Abby, you *do* deserve it. You were willing to stay a beast for me! You have a heart of gold."

My eyes fill with tears. "Not always. Sometimes I can be pretty beastly. I've done some terrible things."

"People make mistakes," Mike says. "But a few mistakes don't make a person a monster. No one can be nice all the time."

"Beauty is!" I say.

"But maybe I shouldn't be," Beauty says. She takes off her veil. "I almost got married just to be nice. That doesn't seem very smart. You should get married because it makes you happy."

Mike nods. "I figured out what makes me happy — being a beast! You need to figure out what makes you happy, too, Beauty."

"Books make me happy," she says wistfully.

Oh! "Maybe you should become a librarian or a bookseller!" I exclaim. "You're really good at recommending books."

"You are welcome to take all the books in the basement," Mike says.

Beauty's eyes shine, but then she shakes her head.

"I can't be a librarian," she says. "I have to help the orphans. And the soup kitchen. And Grumpy Great-Grandma. And I have to take care of my dad's cottage."

"You've taken care of the cottage for years," I say. "Let your sisters have a turn. Maybe it's time to take care of yourself."

"Maybe," Beauty echoes. She looks around, from me to Jonah to Prince to Mike. "I guess my first step is taking off the engagement ring," she says. "Ready?"

"Are you sure?" I ask Mike.

"Absolutely," he booms.

Beauty wiggles the ring off her finger.

My skin starts to sizzle. It feels as if I'm sitting under a heat lamp at a restaurant. After a few seconds, my face stops sizzling. I touch my cheek. It's smooth.

I look at Mike.

Fur is growing on his face and arms, and he's getting taller and taller. Mr. Beast is turning back into his beastly self. He stretches his arms above his head and he grins, showing off his fangs.

"That feels much better," he says happily. "I'm me! Mike is such a boring name anyway. Good-bye, Mike. Hellooo, Mr. Beast!"

It worked. We're back to normal.

Suddenly, the front door smashes open.

"What is going on in here?" demands Jax the fairy with a nasty smile.

I jump. "We switched back. You said if they broke their engagement, we would switch back."

"Hmm," says Jax. He runs his fingers through his purple hair. "Yes, I did say that, didn't I? But that was before you people didn't invite me to the party! You invited everyone but me! That wasn't very nice! Don't you know that fairies get mad when they're not invited to parties? Now you will all be punished. Everyone here will become beasts."

"What?" I say, panicked. "No! You can't do that!"

He takes out his yo-yo and starts swirling it over his head. "Yes, I can! *One beast, two beasts, now a few; You should be a beast, and you and you and you!*"

"Not again!" I say as I feel my body stretch and the fur sprout on my face and hands.

I watch in horror as the same fur sprouts across Jonah's and Beauty's faces.

I hear anguished screams from the Great Hall. Them too?

The fairy swirls his yo-yo around his fingers and cackles. "Now *this* is a party!"

✳ chapter nineteen ✳

Flying Fur

"Stop it, Jax!" Mr. Beast yells.

But Jax just laughs.

All the guests pour out of the Great Hall.

There are beasts in top hats. Beasts in long dresses. Beasts in short dresses. Beasts in earrings. Beasts in all different shades of fur. Even Prince looks different. He's a little bigger and his fangs are extra-long. They look like walrus tusks.

People are yelling all around us.

"What is happening?"

"Where are two of my fingers?"

"I'm so hairy!"

"I'm so hungry!"

"My feet hurt!"

We are a castle full of angry beasts.

Jax is standing in the middle of the foyer, laughing.

I turn to Jonah. Beast Jonah. Fur is exploding out of his shirt and pants. His suspenders have burst. And look at how tall he is!

"Abby!" Jonah cries. "Help! I'm a beast! I'm so itchy!"

What do I do?

"Jax!" I yell. "You have to turn us BACK!"

"What, Abby?" Mrs. Butler asks me. "You want us to ATTACK?"

I shake my hairy head. "That's not what I said!" Hmm. We *are* a roomful of angry beasts. And Jax is just one purple-haired fairy.

Maybe I *do* want us to attack. But I want us to attack super carefully so he doesn't use his yo-yo on us.

I wave to get the attention of Jonah-beast, Mr. Beast, the Butler-beasts, and Beauty-beast, who somehow manages to still look gorgeous, even in beast form. Then I point to Jax and make a circling motion with my finger, and mouth, *Circle him!*

They do. We do.

Jax is laughing too hard to even notice. Until he's surrounded.

"Give us the yo-yo," I say calmly.

"Or what?" he asks.

"Or you will get eaten by wild beasts," Mr. Beast says. "And we are extremely hungry animals."

"GRRRRRRR," all the beasts in the room say.

Before any of us can attack, Prince-beast pounces on Jax, grabs the yo-yo with his walrus fangs, and scurries back to me.

"Good job, Prince!" I say, scratching behind his beastly ears. "You've certainly earned your seat at the dinner table! Now what do I do to reverse the spell?"

"What does she do?" Mr. Beast snarls at Jax. "Tell her what to do or you are about to be a delicious snack."

Jax pouts. "Just swing it back and forth and make up a rhyme. You guys are no fun."

I swing the yo-yo again and again and say, "Hello, party people . . . go back to normal . . ."

"That doesn't rhyme," Jonah-beast tells me, grabbing the yo-yo with his furry hand. "Let me try. *It's feeling kind of warm, turn back into normal form!*" he cries, and swirls the yo-yo like a lasso.

My skin starts to sizzle again. I touch my cheek. Once again, it's smooth.

"It worked!" I say. I look around. Everyone is back to normal. They're all touching their smooth cheeks.

Everyone except Mr. Beast.

"It didn't work on you, Mr. B," Jonah says.

"That's okay," Mr. Beast replies. "I didn't expect it to. Please don't feel sorry. I accept who I am. And, Jonah — good rhyming."

"Maybe now that you're a reader, you'll become a poet, too," Beauty says.

Jonah puffs his chest with pride.

There's a loud knock on the door.

"Come in!" we all yell.

"Hello?" says a voice. A girl steps inside, closing her umbrella. She looks familiar. Spiky blond hair, freckles . . . Oh! It's Freckles.

"Sorry I'm late," she says sheepishly. "I had to close up the shop and —"

Freckles looks up and stops talking. Her eyes meet Mr. Beast's. They stare at each other. And stare.

"Hello," she says slowly.

"Hello," he says.

They can't take their eyes off each other.

Freckles approaches me and pokes my shoulder. "Hi, Abby. Who's your handsome friend?"

Does she mean Mr. Beast? She does! What's that other expression that Nana loves? Oh! "Beauty is in the eye of the beholder!" Meaning beauty is different for different people.

Freckles thinks Mr. Beast is handsome just the way he is.

"It's Mr. Beast," I say.

She blushes. "He's the man Mrs. Butler shops for? The one who's marrying Beauty?"

"That's him," I say. "But the engagement is off."

Her eyes light up. "Really?"

I nod. Then I pepper Freckles with questions. "Do you like to play cards?" I ask her.

"Yes," she says.

"Would you rather live in the countryside or in Town?"

"Countryside. Town is loud."

"And finally: Are you allergic to cheese?" I ask her.

"Of course not," she says. "I run a cheese shop!"

"Oh! Right! Mr. Beast!" I call out. "There's someone I want you to meet!"

He swaggers over. "Hello," he says with a bow. He offers her his arm.

Freckles giggles, takes it, and the two of them walk off, chattering.

"What was *that*?" Jonah asks.

Beauty chuckles. "I think it was love at first sight."

Mr. and Mrs. Butler carry Jax out the door.

"Put me down!" he hollers.

"No, I will not bring you to Town," Mr. Butler says.

"We're not chauffeurs!" Mrs. Butler adds.

With that, they drop Jax on the doormat and turn back into the castle.

"I need my yo-yo!" Jax yells. "It's very powerful! And it's raining outside! And I don't have an umbrella! It's not fair! Everyone else has it so easy and my life is so hard!"

"*You* made your life hard," I tell him through the open door. "You shouldn't have turned Mike into Mr. Beast. You shouldn't have turned *me* into a beast. You shouldn't have turned all the guests into beasts! You need to apologize."

"No way am I apologizing! I don't apologize for anything!" Jax hollers. "You can tell my cousin I'm not sorry for what happened in Wallenta!"

Huh? What is he talking about? "What happened in Wallenta?" I ask. "What is Wallenta? Who's your cousin?"

Ignoring me, Jax gets up and stomps his way through puddles and into the forest, while muttering to himself.

When I'm about to close the door, I spot an older man approaching the castle. His hair is gray and his eyes look weary and tired.

"Excuse me," he says. "It's raining and I'm lost. Can I come in?"

Hmm. I'm not supposed to let strangers into a house. But what if he's a wedding guest?

My internal debate is interrupted by Beauty. She yells "Dad!" and runs into his arms.

Dad?

"Honey!" Beauty's father says, looking shocked and delighted.

"I thought you were on a work trip," Beauty says.

"I was," Beauty's dad says, patting her hair. "I was on my way home. But I got lost. And it started to rain. This castle was the only place around for miles. What are you doing here?"

This all sounds familiar . . . oh!

"Jonah, look!" I cry, pointing to Beauty's father. "It's the beginning of the original story! Beauty's dad — the merchant — is lost and looking for a place to stay!"

"Does the whole story start over again, then?" Jonah asks me. "Is that how this works?

"No," I say sadly. I can't believe Jonah still doesn't have his fairy tale memories back. We've been here over a day. "Now . . . well, we go home."

"Good-bye, everyone!" Jonah calls out to the guests. "It was nice to meet you! But my parents are going to wake up soon and we have to get back to Smithville through the magic mirror upstairs!"

The guests look a bit confused. Understandably.

"I'll come see you guys off," Beauty says, looping her arms through ours.

Mr. and Mrs. Butler take Beauty's dad to get something to eat.

We find Mr. Beast in the kitchen with Freckles. They're making mac and cheese.

Cute.

"We have to go," I tell them. "But it was really nice to meet both of you!"

"How will you get home?" Mr. Beast asks.

"The magic mirror upstairs should do the trick," I say.

"We'll walk you up, then," Freckles says.

"I'll meet you there in a moment," Mr. Beast says. "There's something I have to do."

Beauty, Freckles, Jonah, and I climb the stairs and walk into the sitting room.

"I'll miss you," I say to Beauty. "Please take care of yourself. Not just everyone else."

She nods. "I'll try."

Mr. Beast bursts into the room. "These are for your mom," he says to me and Jonah. "For her birthday." He hands me the biggest, most beautiful bouquet of roses I've ever seen.

Aw. "Wow. Thank you," I say.

"I'll miss you, Mr. B!" Jonah cries, and throws his arms around him.

"You too, little man. You too."

"And thanks for the books," Jonah tells Beauty. "I can't wait to read the rest."

"Enjoy," she says.

The clock in my parents' bedroom says 6:43. We have two

minutes, home time, until their alarm goes off. Ten minutes in fairy tale time. Perfect.

"So how does this work?" Jonah asks me. "We just knock and step through?"

"Yep," I say. "Follow me." I take Jonah's hand and pick up Prince. "Good-bye, everyone!"

"Good-bye!" Beauty, Mr. Beast, and Freckles call out.

I knock once. Twice. Three times.

We wait.

Nothing happens.

Uh-oh. I try again. Once. Twice. Three times.

"How long does it usually take?" Beauty asks.

"Not this long," I admit.

"Let me try," Jonah says.

He knocks once. Twice. Three times.

Nothing.

"Abby," Jonah says. "I don't think the mirror is the way home."

The time on my parents' alarm clock changes to 6:44.

Now we're in trouble.

✳ chapter twenty ✳

Is There Another Way?

his isn't working," I finally admit. "The mirror isn't going to take us home." I feel like kicking myself. Why didn't I test the mirror? Why did I just assume it would work? Ahhhh!

"Then what will?" Mr. Beast asks.

"I don't know!" I feel panicked. "It's usually something magical. What else is magical? We have to knock on everything magical! Everyone knock on everything!"

We knock on the walls. We knock on the doors. We knock on the closets. We even knock on the teapots just in case. Nothing works.

The clock changes to 6:45.

BEEEEEEE —

A loud BEEEEEEP rings through the room. And continues to ring. And ring.

"What is that?" Mr. Beast asks, blocking his ears. "It's horrible!"

"It's my parents' alarm clock," I say. "Which means we are out of time!"

"There has to be another way home," Jonah says. "What else around here is magical?"

I think hard. "The yo-yo!" I exclaim. "The yo-yo is magical! Where is it?"

"In my pocket!" Jonah says.

"Jonah," I say. "You were going to bring the yo-yo home? Are you crazy? Do you know how much damage that could have done? You can't bring things home from fairy tales!"

"But I'm bringing home the books! And the roses! And you said Prince came from a fairy tale!"

"That's different," I say. "Kind of."

Jonah takes the yo-yo out of his pocket and tosses it to Beauty. "You can keep it."

"Just don't let Jax get his hands on it," I tell her. Something niggles at the back of my mind. "Mr. Beast? Jax mentioned something about his cousin and Wallenta. Do you know what he was talking about? You're not his cousin, are you?"

He wrinkles his furry forehead. "Me? No."

"He said . . ." My voice trails off. "He said I should tell his cousin he wasn't sorry about what happened in Wallenta. Who was he talking about?"

"I don't know," Mr. Beast says. "I've never heard of Wallenta."

Weird.

"So what do I do?" Beauty asks.

I reach over and lightly push my fingers against the yo-yo in her hand. It swings lightly.

"If we get stuck here, it could be tragic," Jonah chants. *"Come on, yo-yo, and do your magic!"*

I push it again. And a third time. Suddenly, the yo-yo starts to swing faster. Back and forth and back and forth until it is going around and around in a perfect circle. The air around it feels electric.

"Something's happening," Beauty says.

"It's working," I say. "Ready, Jonah?"

He's staring intently at the yo-yo. His eyes are turning a light shade of purple.

"Jonah?" I ask.

"Abby," he says. "What are crownies?"

"Huh?" I ask.

"Have I ever eaten something called a crownie?" He licks his lips.

"Yes!" I shriek. "You have! When we were in the story of *Cinderella*! We called brownies crownies! Are you remembering crownies?"

"Yes," he says. "Who's Felix?"

Hurrah! "He's Sleeping Beauty's brother! You found him really annoying!"

Jonah turns to me. "Oh yeah. I remember him. He *was* annoying."

I forcibly swing Jonah's face back toward the yo-yo. "Don't look away, Jonah. Your memories are coming back! The yo-yo is reverse hypnotizing you!"

Jonah's eyes turn an even darker purple. "We were able to breathe underwater?"

"We were!" I shout. "We really were!"

"It's all coming back to me!" Jonah screams while the yo-yo spins faster and faster and Jonah's eyes get purpler and purpler. "Abby! Maryrose never said you were in charge when we visit fairy tales!"

Oops.

A big puff of gold smoke blows out of the yo-yo, and Jonah's eyes go back to normal. Suddenly, the mirror behind us turns purple.

"The mirror," I say. "It's glowing. Jonah? Are you done?"

Speechless, he nods. "Yup. I remember everything. And, Abby —"

The mirror is starting to hiss. "Later, Jonah! We have to go."

I pick Prince up, take my brother's hand, and together we step inside the portal.

✳ chapter twenty-one ✳

Home, Sweet Home

We fall onto the floor in a heap. Prince wriggles out of my grasp and barks.

"We made it," I say. "Plus, we're in the basement! Jonah, are you okay?"

Jonah nods, but he looks completely dazed. "My brain feels like it's going to explode."

"It's all the memories," I say. "Come, we have to get into bed really quietly! And quickly! Mom and Dad's alarm already went off. That means they're getting out of bed any minute. Time is back to normal now. Go, go, go!"

"But —"

I pick up Prince and we run — very, very quietly — up the stairs.

Our parents' door is closed, but we can hear their muffled voices.

"Abby —" Jonah starts.

Later! I mouth, and I jump into my room and gently close my door behind me. At the same time, I hear my parents' door open.

I dive under my covers.

"Good morning, sweetheart," my mom says, opening my door and coming inside. "Time to get up." She gently pulls my covers off. "Abby!" she exclaims, ogling my outfit. "You're all dressed up!"

Huh? Uh-oh. I'm still wearing my purple satin dress!

Oh! I know! "Of course I am," I say, hopping out of bed. "It's your surprise birthday party! Come on in, Jonah! Surprise, Mom!"

Prince bounds in, his bow tie still on. *"Ruff!"*

Jonah rushes in next, bouquet of roses in hand, suspenders and bow tie still a mess. "Happy birthday, Mom!"

"Oh, wow," she says. "Look at you guys! And those flowers are beautiful! I'm speechless!" Her eyes tear up. "You kids are the sweetest. But where did you get those outfits?"

Hmm. "Nana sent them for us," I say. "Don't you remember?"

She scrunches her eyebrows together. "No."

I shrug. "You *are* a year older. Your memories must be getting fuzzy."

My mom laughs. "Is that for me, too?" she asks, pointing to the wrapped painting on my desk.

"Oh," I say. "Yeah. But it's not . . ." I'm about to say that it's not good. But maybe that doesn't matter. Maybe what matters is that I did my best. That it came from the heart. So what if I'm not as good an artist as Penny? I'm good at other stuff. Mr. Beast accepted who he is. Maybe it's time for me to accept who I am. "Here you go," I say, handing it to her.

"Oooh," she says, unwrapping it. "Abby! It's wonderful. So much color! I absolutely love it," she says. And when I look at her shining eyes, the funny thing is, I know that she means it. Maybe beauty really is in the eye of the beholder.

"Thanks, Mom," I say, my own eyes tearing up now.

My mom squeezes my shoulder. "Let's go show Dad. He's downstairs making birthday waffles."

Jonah raises his eyebrows at me. "I need to talk to Abby for a sec."

"You can talk to her at the table," my mom says, ushering him out of my room. "C'mon, I don't want you to be late for school."

I wait for them to head downstairs before running over to my jewelry box.

"Prince!" I hear my mom say. "Sorry, buddy, but you do not get to sit at the table. Even if it's a special occasion."

I giggle. Poor Prince.

I look at my jewelry box. There's Beauty! She's standing in front of what used to be the cheese shop. But now instead, it says LIBRARY. Beauty's holding a pile of books, smiling a huge smile, and looking more beautiful than ever, because she's truly happy. I'm so proud of her!

And wait a minute — there's another image next to her. It's Mr. Beast! With his arm around Freckles. They're standing in front of the castle where a sign reads THE B&B: BED AND (EXTRA-CHEESY) BREAKFAST.

I am so proud of *them*.

I'm still not very proud of myself. I know we are all part beauty and part beast, but I want to try to be more beauty than beast.

And maybe there's a way I can make that happen.

"Penny, can I talk to you?" I say before art class. "In private?"

Penny follows me over to the side of the hallway. "What's up?"

I take a very big breath. "You were right," I say. "Yesterday. It wasn't an accident. I spilled the water on your painting on purpose. And I want to say I'm sorry."

She jerks back in shock. "But why would you do that?" she snaps. "I worked hard on it."

I hang my head. "I know. And it was beautiful. And I was jealous. You are really good at painting."

"And you're not," she says.

"Yeah." Thanks for rubbing it in.

She leans against a locker. "I can't believe you admitted it. My mom told me you were probably jealous."

My cheeks heat up. She discussed me with her mom? I'm so embarrassed. I swallow. Hard. "Your mom was right," I say. "Can you forgive me? I'll help in any way I can."

"I don't need help with art," she says. She opens her mouth and then closes it.

"What?" I ask, leaning closer. "Please let me make it up to you."

"Well . . . do you think you could help me with geography? I'm having a hard time understanding the map. And you seem good at it."

"Of course," I say. "Any time!"

Penny sighs. "Sometimes I'm kind of jealous of you, too, Abby. School comes so easily to you. It's harder for me."

Did she say she was jealous of me? Of *me*?

I blink at her in surprise.

"I — well, I guess we're all good at different things," I say. "But I am sorry about your painting."

"It's okay. Just remind me not to put water next to you in art class," she says, her eyes twinkling.

I blush but I also laugh. I spot Robin watching us from inside the classroom. I wave.

Robin gives us a hopeful smile.

We smile back.

"Should we go inside?" Penny asks.

"Let's go," I say, and take a step toward class.

"Abby!" Jonah says, appearing at my side. We go to the same school, but I almost never see him between classes since his grade is in another part of the building. He grabs on to my arm. "I've been trying to talk to you all morning."

"What's going on? What's wrong? Did you lose your memories again?" I ask in a hushed tone.

"No," he says. He wiggles his eyebrows. "The opposite."

"What does that mean?" I ask.

166

"I know what Wallenta is," he says.

"You do? What?"

"It's the kingdom that Maryrose and Jax grew up in."

"It is?" I ask. "They grew up in the same kingdom?"

"Yes," he says. "They're cousins! When Jax said he wasn't going to apologize about what happened to his cousin in Wallenta, he wasn't talking about Mr. Beast. He was talking about Maryrose!"

Wow. Finally, we know something about Maryrose! We know where she grew up. And that she has a mean, jealous cousin!

The second bell rings.

Wait a sec. "But, Jonah, how did you find that out?" I ask.

"Because it wasn't just *my* memories that came back," he says, walking away from me and smiling mischievously. "I got some of Maryrose's, too."

"What?" I ask incredulously.

He taps his head. "Maryrose's memories! In here!"

And with those words, he disappears down the hall, leaving me staring after him in amazement.

Don't miss Abby and Jonah's next adventure,
where they fall into the tale of *The Frog Prince*!

Look for:

Whatever After #8: ONCE UPON A FROG

acknowledgments

Once upon a time there was an author who was very grateful for:

Aimee Friedman, Laura Dail, Tamar Rydzinski, Deb Shapiro, Becky Amsel, Abby McAden, David Levithan, Ellie Berger, Lori Benton, Tracy van Straaten, Jennifer Ung, Bess Braswell, Whitney Steller, Robin Baily Hoffman, Sue Flynn, Emily Cullings, Elizabeth Krych, Joy Simpkins, Elizabeth Parisi, Lizette Serrano, Emily Heddleson, Emily Jenkins, Cassie Homer, Elissa Ambrose, Aviva Mlynowski, Larry Mlynowski, Louisa Weiss, Robert Ambrose, the Dalven-Swidlers, the Finkelstein-Mitchells, the Steins, the Greens, the Adamses, the Wolfes, the Mittlemans, the Bilermans, Courtney Sheinmel, Anne Heltzel, Lauren Myracle, Emily Bender, Targia Alphonse, Rose Brock, Jess Braun, Lauren Kisilevsky, Bonnie Altro, Robin Afrasiabi, Jess Rothenberg, Stephen Barbara, Jennifer E. Smith, Robin Wasserman, Elizabeth Eulberg, Maureen Johnson, Adele Griffin, Milan Popelka, Leslie Margolis, Maryrose Wood, Tara Altebrando, Sara Zarr, Ally Carter, Jennifer Barnes, Alan Gratz, Avery Carmichael, Maggie Marr, Jeremy Cammy, and Farrin Jacobs.

Extra love and extra thanks to Chloe, Anabelle, and Todd.

Whatever After readers: You are all beauty queens.

about the author

Sarah Mlynowski is the author of the Magic in Manhattan series, *Gimme a Call*, and a bunch of other books for tweens, teens, and grown-ups. Originally from Montreal, Sarah now lives in the kingdom of Manhattan with her very own prince charming and their fairy tale–loving daughters. Visit Sarah online at www.sarahm.com and find her on Instagram and Twitter @sarahmlynowski.